THE HIGH COST
OF MACARONI

A Novel

by
Ryan George Kittleman

THE HIGH COST OF MACARONI

Ghost-like I paced round the haunts of my childhood,
Earth seem'd a desert I was bound to traverse,
Seeking to find the old familiar faces.

- Charles Lamb

What shall I do with this absurdity —
O heart, O troubled heart

- William Butler Yeats

Prologue

EVERY DAY, IT seems, another building collapses in Old Dutch City. As its name implies, the place bears the scars of age. Prolonged neglect has hastened the gradual withering that all corporeal matter must inevitably suffer. Time plus neglect: a simple formula that takes no account of size, location, or significance — to history, or to me. Nothing is exempt, everything is vulnerable. Thus do city blocks — neighborhoods even — crumble and succumb, leaving only footprints in gravel, scattered across the landscape like so many holes in a tattered tapestry.

As I think about it now, it's with some amazement that I realize many of these buildings have been vacant my entire life.

Decades and decades without a tenant, longer still without anyone to care for their fate. When I was a child, my parents and grandparents would recall their prior lives- a department store here, a hat shop there- but I viewed them more simply:

Empty.

Rotten.

Home.

And yet, if I were to sort through the debris, who knows what I would learn of the varied fortunes of those who inhabited Old Dutch City over the centuries? Whatever memories I attached to these locations were merely products of their vacancy. For instance, the old pencil factory was never operational in my lifetime, and when I saw its faded sign, pockmarked as if gnawed on by an anxious student, it meant only that the river was straight ahead. Then, loitering along the river's edge, bored and stoned, I would look back and ponder the decrepit hulk I had passed to get there.

To me, these edifices may have been nothing more than trusty way-finders, but even then I always felt a certain sense of loss whenever one finally toppled. Another guidepost gone, the topography of my youth forever altered once more. Was this nothing more than nostalgic humbug? Perhaps.

My hometown, in short, is a dump. When I left Old Dutch City ten years ago with a single suitcase and a one-way ticket west, I vowed never to return. I was resolved to fill that vacant lot in my mind with something — anything — else.

Then, out of the blue, Oisin's letter arrived. Seeing as it lacked postage, a proper envelope, and even legible penmanship, this was nothing short of a miracle. The letter bore the weight of a friendship gone but never wholly forgotten, and as I sifted through the linguistic artifacts of a relationship as lost to time as the ruins of my youth, I realized that it was an invitation of sorts.

Old Dutch City, it claimed, was celebrating its Quadricentennial — that is to say, it was turning four hundred years old — and I was invited to join the festivities. I should have known better, but for whatever reason, Oisin's perplexing, semi-coherent chicken scratch swept me up in a wave of nostalgia powerful enough to overwhelm any determination I had to swim through it.

Sitting alone in my tiny but nevertheless expensive studio apartment three thousand miles away, I thought, "Why not?"

Why *not* return to the shabby streets of that once-proud old mare? If nothing else, its sheer ability to survive was worth toasting. And despite the distance I had traveled, I wondered how far I had actually come. In any event, I knew that I wouldn't be around to honor another such anniversary. Judging from its state of affairs, I had my doubts that the city would be either.

So I packed up the very suitcase I had left with a decade earlier and purchased the return ticket I had successfully deferred for so long. Heading for the airport, I thought all the while of the countless empty buildings of Old Dutch City. I never imagined that, within twenty-four hours, another of those buildings would be gone, and that I would be directly responsible for its destruction.

The Good Woman's Final Voyage

IT ALL BEGAN with a ship called *Goede Vrouw* (The Good Woman). The voyage commenced in 1614. On behalf of the Dutch East India Company, the famed explorer Lars Hendriksen and his crew of rogues and wastrels launched the lady down the Super-Sargasso River in search of the lost city of Norumbega. Yet the lost city preferred not to be found, and after months of fruitless travel and the onset of scurvy and dysentery, the crew grew mutinous. The conspirators' plan to divert the ship toward sunnier climes, however, was to remain as speculative as Norumbega's existence. Never one to suffer scoundrels lightly, Captain Hendriksen banished them to a rocky cove near the site where Old Dutch City stands today before sailing off to continue his own pointless adventure.

Led by a young steward named Kiliaen Van Eck, these erstwhile mariners quickly refashioned themselves as intrepid pioneers. They did everything they thought pioneers should do: clear terrain, plant crops, erect a stockade. While no one knows for sure why Van Eck dubbed the new settlement *Schytt Bergie* (Dung Hill), it was likely inspired, at least in part, by the sailors' dysentery. This appellation would last until the British annexed the bustling little town several decades later, politely renaming it Old Dutch City.

Four hundred years later, the *Good Woman* began her final voyage guided by Captain Oisin Fitzpatrick. Actually, it was only a full-scale replica commissioned for the Quadricentennial, but if you didn't look too closely you could almost pretend it was the original.

Oi's instructions were clear: at midnight, I was to await his arrival "under that rusty bridge where we used to get high." There was no point asking why he preferred such a clandestine rendezvous — for better or for worse, Oi always had his reasons. And so, right on time, I arrived at that creaky old bridge, shivering. Oi, obviously, was nowhere to be seen.

Soon I began to feel uneasy and overexposed; I considered repairing to the nearest tavern. Should someone inquire why I was there, standing by myself in that woebegone stretch of the city, I'd be utterly at a loss for an answer. To any respectable people passing by, I would appear to be merely another hustler, john, or addict.

Keep driving, honey, they'd say to each other. *Just another loser.*

Of course, there were no respectable people passing by. The silence was unnerving. How quiet it was! The stillness alone was enough to make me feel as though I was doing something wrong just by being there. I would have even welcomed the appearance of the police; at least then, I'd have less to fear from the unseemly characters I imagined lurking in the shadows. Nevertheless, I was feeling more annoyed than scared, and somehow very out-of-place in these formerly familiar surroundings.

There was nothing to do but stare at the string of connected iron Xs that spanned the length of the river. What a stupid bridge, I thought. Nothing but two thousand feet of rusted scrap metal. In school, we were taught that the bridge had been built by a kindly industrialist with the aim of cornering the fur trade. At the time, it went unmentioned that this same captain of industry was also known for frequenting — and frequently murdering — local prostitutes.

Eventually, I came to see the bridge as an emblem of all the dirty dealing and *sub rosa* depravity that's always defined this city. My mother once told me that, in the days when the bridge still needed guarding, my great-grandfather served as the night watchman of that hideous span. What became of him? I asked. Well, one night, when he was in hot pursuit of two juvenile delinquents, he was flattened by a bootlegger's train. One minute it's, *Hey, you punks, get over here! I order you to halt!* The next, splat. They didn't even give him a plaque.

Needless to say, I was in a somewhat skeptical state of mind when, suddenly, the bow of the *Good Woman* cut through the evening fog. Crafted from solid oak, this beauty emerged from the mists double-masted, broad-bottomed and, as they say, high-pooped. From the foremast, the same orange-, white-, and blue-barred flag of the Netherlands that the ship bore when last she sailed these waters fluttered proudly.

In contrast to this historic tri-color banner, the somewhat curious flag of Old Dutch City — on which a corncob and a potato were awkwardly arranged in resemblance of male genitalia — had been hoisted up the mainmast. The impression made by these concupiscent vegetables was in no way softened by the fat beaver and half-naked Indian brave they were sandwiched between. Just as the USA has its Old Glory, in ODC we have the Old Cock & Balls. No one's sure exactly what the founders intended with their choice, but it's certainly given generations of perverts plenty of cause for bawdy speculation.

The vessel was, of course, the striking and lifelike replica of the *Goede Vrouw*, but given the late hour and foreboding atmosphere, my first thought was that it was *The Flying Dutchman* stalking its ghostly course. The melancholy wail that emerged from the deck only strengthened these suspicions.

As I should have known, it was just Oi on a drunken joyride. I recognized him as soon as I saw him, owing mainly to the wild shock of copper hair that still burned bright atop his head. Spotting me from afar, he yelled, "All abroad!" and waved a silly wave.

"Come ride this *Good Woman* 'til the broad daylight!"

I shrugged. I was a weak swimmer, and the distance between us was hopelessly far. Ever resourceful, Oi scoured the deck until he came up with a ring buoy (an anachronistic concession to modern safety regulations, I assumed). Much to my surprise, he was able to hurl that sucker clear onto the shore.

I gave Oi a thumbs-up, then stared blankly at the float. I still had my reservations. First, the Super-Sargasso River is notoriously cold and even more notoriously polluted; and second, I would be joining Oi on a boat that I knew with a high degree of certainty he had no right to be on. Despite my misgivings, anything seemed preferable to continuing to stand underneath the bridge. So I grabbed the ring and waded out into the dark and icy waters.

I should note that my approach to swimming involves a lot of wild flailing. While this may create a frothy wake, it does little to actually propel me forward. Oi figured this out and found a second buoy, this one attached to a rope, which he used to successfully reel me in.

And so, sopping wet and still a little wobbly, I was finally able to greet my old friend. The years seemed to have had little effect on Oisin. He was still boyishly handsome, his smile still flashed like a broken neon sign, the rounded belly on his otherwise wiry frame signaled he remained a big league drinker, and his scabby knuckles confirmed he was still the heavyweight brawler I well remember.

"Ahoy landlubber!" he said, taking my hand in his. "Come warm those sodden bones of yours with a toasty drink!"

I should have known. Even for a "touching reunion," Oi was ready to go straight to the booze, always. Now, using the various gimcracks on the deck, he had even set up an impromptu bar; given the choice of a Hot Flip (a mix of rum and beer) or an apple toddy (a sweet drink made from cider and brandy), I chose the toddy.

Taking hold of the captain's wheel, Oi shouted back to me, "I knew you'd come! Sure as shit on a truck-stop wall! I invited everyone from the old crew, you know — but only you showed! It's like I always say, you can separate a man from his hometown, but you can't separate a man from his hometown! Or something."

I wrung out my socks and considered my response. I was trying to determine the best way to inquire about just how and why we were on this mock-historical vessel in the middle of the river in the middle of the night when Oi, as usual, beat me to the punch.

"It's like they were just begging me to steal this thing!" he yelled. "You know how much they spent on this hunk of junk? A million smackeroos! And all because they wanted some big surprise to haul out for the Quadricentennial! Can't you see it now? All those assholes in their clogs and bonnets, dancing around,

sticking tulips up their asses, when all of a sudden —
hey look, it's a big boat!

"That's the surprise? Big whoop. Well, if maritime
make-believe is their definition of fun, I thought, why
should they have all of it? Surely, as a life-long resident
of this fair burg, I should take her out for a test drive
before the big day! So that's what I did."

I watched nervously as he steered the ship with one
hand while hoisting a hot flip with the other. "Ever
been sailing before?" I asked.

"Never once!" he laughed. "But hey, it ain't so hard.
Look, the sails do all the work. All I have to do is stand
here like some hotshot and wait to hear the people cry,
'Lo! There goes Oisin passing in the night, rousing the
ghosts and exercising the demons!'"

"I believe the expression is *exorcising* the demons," I
replied.

"Sure, but really, what's the diff? Wouldn't hurt me
to work out a bit more either way. Look at this belly
I've put on since I left the joint! Back then, all I did was
work out, but not anymore, no sir. Now I've got better
things to do," he said, taking a quaff from his flask.
"Anyway, who cares? A little exercise never hurt
nobody."

"Except when someone gets hurt exercising."

"True, true. Always the wise one, Kip. But why are
we even worrying about this now — we're sailing,
baby! Take a load off, my man. Settle in, cool out, and
smoke 'em if ya got 'em."

I pulled my cigarettes from my pocket. Like everything else on my person, the pack was soaked beyond use. I tossed the limp box into the river.

"Place looks the same as ever," I said, scanning the twinkling skyline of Old Dutch City as the *Good Woman* cruised downriver.

"Look closer! There's so much more to it these days!" Oi exclaimed. He was practically hanging off the railing as he pointed to a spot in the distance. "That's where the original stockade was, you know. And that state house up on the hill, that's where the fort used to be. Fort Dung Hill! Can you stand it? I swear, the only thing this place still has going for it is its sense of humor!"

I tried to imagine it, but couldn't. A disorderly mess of buildings piled on top of each other obscured the image Oi was trying to conjure. I could picture only the streets as I remembered them, converging at all angles, creating a tortuous maze dotted with a jumble of decaying structures: hulking glass columns that spoke of power; sharp spires that spoke of faith; and slim, stylish cement towers, dated odes to modernism that spoke of a failed vision for the future. But none of it spoke to me. If that forlorn skyline suggested anything, it wasn't that this was the oldest European settlement in America, only that it was the most decrepit. There were simply too many holes, each a reminder of a building that was no longer there.

"Do you realize that when Fort Dung Hill was

built," Oi continued, "*Don Quixote* was still a new book? Cervantes' latest! And everyone was talking about this play that just premiered called *Hamlet*! Rembrandt was just a baby and Voltaire hadn't even been born yet! Did you know that ODC is older than the telescope, the cuckoo clock, flush toilets, and bifocals?"

"Well, sure, but you know what's older than all those things? Scurvy. Dysentery. Being old doesn't make something good. There are plenty of old things we'd be better off without. Is preserving something that isn't even worth keeping really more important than thinking about the future?"

"Pish. Posh. Who has time for the future? I, for one, find that the past has more than enough to offer!"

"So I've noticed," I replied bitterly.

Oi must have noticed my tone, as he waited a moment before speaking again. When he resumed, the merriment was gone from his voice. "Can I ask you something, Kip? Are you ever sad you left?"

"Not really," I replied truthfully.

After that, Oi and I just sat in silence, sipping our drinks and looking in opposite directions. Her full press of canvas spread to the wind, the *Good Woman* continued to glide downriver.

Before long, we picked up a windward breeze and began cruising at a nice clip. Oi took this smooth sailing as a sign that, in mere minutes, he had transformed himself from novice to master and disappeared into the officer's cabin. Since he didn't say anything, I could only assume he was making a trip to the chamber pot. Unfortunately, his departure coincided with a particularly nasty crosscurrent. As we reached the city's north end, the ship pulled sharply toward the shore. I scrambled to correct the wheel, but there was bigger trouble ahead: a railroad trestle was rapidly approaching.

Pants around his ankles, Oi came running out of the cabin, yelling: "What happened? What happened!" He tried desperately to right the ship, but there was no hope that the *Good Woman* could be diverted from her fatal path. "We're fucked," he said. "We have to jump ship."

I looked down at the murky waters rushing by. "I don't think I can swim that far," I said.

"You got no choice, Kip. This ship is toast."

Demonstrating that his priorities were still in place, Oi immediately tossed the flasks of flip and toddy overboard; with a dull thud, they landed in a clump of weeds on the nearby shore. He then climbed the port side railing and prepared to jump.

"Come on, man," he shouted, extending his hand to me. But I was frozen in place.

"I think I'm just gonna ride it out," I said, stupidly.

Without any deliberation, Oi jumped down, scooped me up in a bear hug, and heaved us both over the side.

As soon as we hit the water, I instinctively began to flail. "Stop it!" Oi said, grasping me tighter in response.

"Quit moving!"

I went limp and let Oi take over. In spite of the extra weight he was carrying, he managed to battle the current forcefully and fluidly. I looked on, helpless; in regular intervals, my head bobbed in and out of the water. Each time I resurfaced the dim lights of the city had grown closer. After what seemed like an eternity, (in fact, it was not even a minute), we were finally back on solid ground.

"Guess we managed to exercise those demons after all," said Oi, between gasps, before collapsing in a heap. "You still breathing, Kip?"

"I swallowed some water, but other than that I'm fine," I replied. I decided not to bring up the emasculating blow that my ego had just suffered.

"How's it taste?"

"Terrible," I said, trying to spit the muck from my mouth.

"Sounds like we could both use some liquid refreshment," Oi answered. "Mind passing the flip?"

As I scanned the shore for the flask, I saw that the ship was still careening down the river. At last, before my very eyes, the *Good Woman* made her date with the tall, dark, and handsome bridge.

The initial crash shattered the figurehead on the prow; from bow to stern, the ship's beams began to shatter. As she smashed against the trestle, a hole was torn into the vessel's side, and soon she began to take on water rapidly.

"This place has too many bridges," I said.

"But," Oi replied, "one less boat."

As if we hadn't destroyed enough already, the ship's mainmast — a thick, towering post some thirty feet high — then snapped like a twig as the *Good Woman* sunk into the river. Falling with a terrible groan, the mast came crashing down onto Trinity Church, a quaint waterfront chapel.

"The Dutchman's wail," I observed mournfully.

"There goes Old Cock & Balls," Oi added as we watched the city's emblem collapse into the pews. "Will its assaults on religion never cease?"

"Maybe we should see this as a metaphor for how the railroads hastened the demise of maritime trade? Or for how industrialization created a more secular society?"

"You do realize we're in deep shit, right?" Oi reminded me.

"I'm doing my best not to think about it."

History Village

LOOKING FOR A place to hide, Oi and I scurried along the riverfront. Soon we came to the delivery bay of a company called Old Dutch Pipe & Nipple (which I choose to assume, for the sake of decency, is a plumbing company). We ducked in to catch our breath.

"We're too exposed," Oi whispered. "We need permanent cover. Or at least *temporary* permanent cover." He scanned our surroundings, then pointed to a rusted fence that stood between us and a dark clearing in the distance. "This way," he said.

As we arrived at the fence, he added, "Trust me on this,"
then gracefully hurdled over it.

Trust me, says the guy who just wrecked a million dollar boat and destroyed a church. Hastily, I considered my options. Then, unable to come up with any alternatives that didn't result in the headline, FORMER RESIDENT ARRESTED AT PIPE & NIPPLE, I too jumped the fence.

We made a quick dash across the broken glass-and-candy-wrapper-strewn field before arriving at the destination Oi had chosen for us; a cheaply fabricated sign identified it as History Village. Until that moment, I had never heard of its existence, and judging by the condition of its grounds, I wasn't alone. It was, Oi explained, yet another project commissioned for the Quadricentennial.

Half-finished, History Village had been laid out to resemble a town square, with each building represented by a thin plywood facade painted to evoke a different period from the history of Old Dutch City. The selections were obvious and uninspired: one block featured an Iroquois longhouse, a Dutch farmhouse, an Irish pub, an Italian market, and a Jewish deli, all incongruously sandwiched together. Of course, the gambling rooms, pool halls, brothels, and other seedy joints that embodied the true historical spirit of the city were nowhere to be found.

This dearth of imagination conspired with a general shortage of funds to create a distinctly surreal impression. My first thought was that we had accidentally stumbled onto the shambolic set of some B-movie. History Village seemed to be ODC's very own version of Spahn Ranch — the former film set where the Manson Family once resided.

"Typical, no?" said Oi, kicking over a plastic replica of a well. "It's the Old Dutch way — announce, then delay, then walk away. I knew this place was doomed from the start. First of all, it's stupid. Second of all, it's ugly. Third of all, it's a lie." To underscore his point, Oi showed me the chintzy plaque affixed to the Irish pub:

In 1847, Eamonn O'Sullivan opened Old Dutch City's first Irish pub at the corner of Hawk Street and Dove Street. Before long, the establishment had grown world famous for its live music and corned beef sandwiches.

"I don't even know where to begin," Oi sighed. "For one thing, Hawk and Dove run parallel to each other, so they never intersect. Alright, well, maybe that could be excused as a meaningless mistake, like a typo or something. But how do you explain the fact that old Eamonn and his famous pub here never even fucking existed? That's right, I looked it up — and found squat! Nothing. Zilch. Same with every other place here! They made up this whole goddamn town! Who needs a real city with a real history when you can create a fake city with a fake history? And you wanna know something else?"

I really didn't.

"To build this lousy Potemkin village they had to tear down a half a dozen buildings. Let me repeat that: they destroyed a real past to make room for their fake one!"

It was certainly ironic, but Oi's ardent protestations and his belabored way of making them did little to rouse my own indignation. The truth is, I didn't entirely disagree with the misguided vision behind History Village. Who cared if parallel streets had been made to intersect or if the drinking holes were conjured from pure imagination? No one seemed to respect the past enough to remember any of it anyway; what difference did it make if they remembered it wrongly? Irish pub, Indian massacre, indigent grandpa torn apart by a train — they're all dead and gone now, buried beneath the indifferent topsoil of the present.

Oi must have noticed my discomfort and attributed it only to the fact that I was still soaking wet and shivering like a soggy dog, because he disappeared into a mock watchhouse and returned carrying two bright orange jumpsuits, like those worn by convicts working along the highway. Eager as I was to get out of my sodden togs, it didn't even seem worth asking what these outfits were doing here or how Oi knew where to find them. Nevertheless, I couldn't deny that, for two fugitives such as ourselves, this was altogether fitting attire.

"Here, put this on," said Oi, as he handed me one of the suits. "I don't want your untimely death in History Village on my head. They'd probably spell your name wrong on the cardboard tombstone."

The desire to be dry had taken away any qualms I felt about stripping down and looking ridiculous, but now Oi seemed reluctant. Inspecting the suit, he muttered, "Never thought I'd have to put on one of these again." His misgivings were apparently too strong for him to ignore, because at last he opted simply to wring out his crusty old shirt and carry on.

In my bright new duds I felt revived, and began marching through History Village and scrutinizing its slapdash storefronts as if I were a general inspecting his troops. And why shouldn't I be a general here, I wondered. Or the mayor. Or a garbage collector. It mattered to absolutely no one, least of all me. In this land of make-believe, it simply didn't matter.

As I surveyed the grounds, I came to a squat little erection that had been painted red and gray. It was identified by a plaque that had been pasted to the facade:

> *The Old Dutch Athenaeum, the oldest public library in the city, has long been considered the heart of intellectual life here in America's oldest European settlement.*

Intellectual life? In Old Dutch City? Even I had to admit that this legend strained credibility. But as I took a moment to indulge my snobbery, I noticed that a curious note had been taped next to the plaque.

Coming Soon: Bread Pudding, it read.

I pondered the message. Over and over I read it, at one point leaning in closer as if the distance were the reason I found it so vexing. Finally I even started rearranging the letters in my head, a fun talent I have that's typically useful only when I find myself staring at some random set of words like "Coming Soon: Bread Pudding."

Icebound, a dingdong romps, I thought. An amusing image, perhaps, but it offered no further insight into the mysterious announcement. At that moment, Oi came up behind me and gave voice to the question at the heart of the matter: "Why would anyone care if bread pudding was coming or not?"

These words seemed to summon some strange specter, because the next thing I knew I could feel a looming presence approach. Soon, its shadow had engulfed me, Oi, the note, even the entire piece of plywood the note was affixed to.

"Let me tell you why," said the apparition in a low and raspy voice.

I must admit that I, for one, was scared shitless — but Oi never lost his cool. Reflexively, he clenched his fist, spun around, and clocked the giant right in the jaw.

"Alright, asshole, tell us," he added, hovering over his fallen foe. The man was out cold. Still, for no good reason, Oi kicked him in the stomach. "We're excited to hear your explanation, Old Man Winter," he prodded.

As it turned out, our very tall interlocutor was vaguely messianic-looking — inasmuch as anyone with long hair, a bushy beard, a flowing robe, and dirty feet looks vaguely messianic. At last, the giant began to stir.

"I reject your violence, as the Prophet Very has instructed," he groaned. "If you must continue your beating, so be it. I fear not, knowing that your own actions are founded in fear."

"You should be afraid, jerk," answered Oi. He seemed to be missing the point.

"You had sought answers about the sign," the man

reminded us. "I merely wished to share the wisdom it imparts. You see, behind these words lies a deeply spiritual message."

I decided to speak up before Oi had a chance to renew his attack. "Please, tell us more," I interjected.

The man lurched to his feet, until he once again towered over us. He smelled terrible.

"The Prophet Very teaches that inevitably does bread grow old and stale," he intoned, "but as their expiry nears, the righteous loaves shall enjoy a rebirth: to become bread pudding is to enjoy an afterlife as sweet and delicious as heaven itself! In his verse, the message could not be clearer: *Fain with swine's food would we our hunger fill; We eat, but 'tis not of the bread from heaven.* Thus, the notice 'Coming Soon: Bread Pudding' reminds us that though death be inevitable, for some a greater destiny awaits."

Having grown tired of the explanation, Oi had wandered off and disappeared behind the facades once more. His absence only seemed to encourage the man. "Are you familiar with the life and works of the Prophet Jones Very?" he asked.

"I can't say that I am," I replied. I looked around desperately for Oi, wishing he would return to protect me.

"In abject poverty was he born, the eldest son of unwed cousins. Yet despite these base beginnings, a distinguished life had been reserved for the Prophet. At Harvard University, he studied literature and, entering

22

its Divinity School upon graduation, subsequently took on the role of tutor. Before long, he had begun to mix with the very cream of New England society. He was even invited to join the Transcendental Club by Emerson himself, who would go on to edit the Prophet's sole volume of essays and verse. One of those rare figures in whom intellect, spirituality, and a poetical disposition are combined, the Prophet Very did not hesitate to promote his radical notions, yet the boldness of his thinking won him few admirers. Even friends could be hostile. Unable to accept the Prophet's revelation that his verse was composed under the influence of the Holy Spirit, Emerson lashed out with a petty assault on his idiosyncratic usage, asking 'Cannot the Spirit parse and spell?'

"The mockery only emboldened the Prophet Very further. These tensions reached their climax one afternoon when, before a class of Harvard undergraduates, the Prophet interrupted his regular lecture — a discussion of the poet Sappho's immortality — to declare Himself the Second Coming of Christ. Rather than embraced for his epiphany and allowed to disclose the proofs that would dispel all objections, the Prophet was swiftly and unceremoniously institutionalized. Though released after a month, he yet remained unwilling to renounce his faith in Himself. For this conviction, he was summarily relieved of his teaching post and expelled from the church at large. For the next forty years, the Prophet lived as a recluse, never again to publish another word."

My bewilderment must have been evident from the blank expression on my face, but the man didn't seem to notice. He took another step toward me, his ratty hair brushing against my shoulder, and continued undeterred. His breath, too, smelled terrible.

"It was as a doctoral candidate in the field of early American literature that I discovered the Prophet Very. The closer I studied his work, the more manifest the truth became: Jones Very indeed *was* the Second Coming, sent to Earth to save mankind. Deeply inspired by this revelation, I promptly left academia and committed myself to an ascetic life of contemplation. And what could be more fitting than to come here to the banks of the Super-Sargasso River, the place where lost things settle. I have even adopted the Prophet's name as my own. You may call me Jones Very, Jr."

"Anselm Kip," I replied, hoping he wouldn't shake my hand. He did.

"I apologize for frightening you and your friend, Mr. Kip. I don't receive many visitors."

I realized that my apprehension had been misplaced. This man was no threat — merely a lonely loon, a gray-haired gentle giant.

At last, Oi decided to reappear. "Yo Kip, check this out," he said, waving a slim, wrinkled manuscript in his hand. "This dude has all sorts of weird shit back here."

Jones Jr. blanched at the sight of Oi handling his

papers so cavalierly. "Please, be careful not to disturb my library," he implored. "It contains years of scholarship and research."

"You call that a library?" Oi replied. "All I saw was a bunch of trash."

"Well, Oi, you know what they say," I began, "One man's trash is another man's—"

"The History of Macaroni and Cheese," Oi interrupted, reading from the front page of the manuscript. Apparently his interest in history didn't extend to pastas, because as soon as he said these words he casually tossed the manuscript to the ground. Jones scrambled to collect the pages before they were blown away.

"Did you not hear me tell you to be careful?" Jones bellowed. "This monograph is a holy text! It synthesizes the teachings of the Prophet and expounds them for our modern age. Only one copy exists — this copy!"

"May I see it?" I asked, extending my hand as non-threateningly as possible. I was curious to read a madman's interpretation of the writings of a madman.

Jones eyed me cautiously. Finally, he handed me the papers. "I hope you find it enlightening," he added sincerely.

Suddenly, I saw a devilish look flash across Oi's face. Whatever idea he was having, I was sure it meant trouble for Jones Very, Jr.

"Hey man," said Oi, approaching Jones with

feigned contrition. "I'm sorry I knocked you on your ass. I'm a good Catholic boy at heart so I'm normally not about to bend in my beliefs easily, but I gotta say — I think you might be onto something with this Macaroni and Cheese deal. Why don't you tell me more about this inbred prophet and his bread pudding and whatnot."

"Of course, my child," replied Jones, clearly unaccustomed to having an audience. "I am at your service."

Oi followed Jones into his library. Positively bushed by the day's events (was it really only that morning that I had left San Francisco?), I decided to stay behind. And so, while Oi engaged in what I'm sure was some very disingenuous gospel study, I curled up next to the mock Iroquois longhouse and read *The History of Macaroni and Cheese* until I drifted into sleep.

The History of Macaroni & Cheese
or,
The Second Gospel of Jones Very
by Rev. Jones Very, Jr.

Article I- Bread

BREAD, THE GIVER of life. It is composed of but two ingredients: flour (which fills our bellies) and water (the very essence of our being). Yet bread's significance transcends its value as mere sustenance. It has become a sacred symbol of fecundity and faith; indeed, bread has become synonymous with life itself.

Early references to this notion can be traced as far back as antiquity:

> *'Rise, and from the heights of the citadel, throw down*
>
> *Among the enemy the last thing you'd wish to yield!'*
>
> *They shook off sleep, and troubled by the strange command,*
>
> *Asked themselves what they must yield,*

unwillingly. It seemed it must be bread.

— Ovid, *Fasti, Book VI* (circa 8 AD)

In invoking "the last thing you'd wish to yield," Ovid is clearly alluding to the sanctity of life. And though this request is troubling to the soldiers, they understand that they must sacrifice themselves in exchange for life everlasting.

Bread symbolism was adopted by early Christians, those great appropriators of belief, as well. To wit:

> *And Jesus said unto them, I am the bread of life.*

— John 6:35

It was not long before the Savior brought this doctrine to its apotheosis:

> *And as they were eating, Jesus took bread, and blessed it, and brake it, and gave it to the disciples, and said,*
> *Take this and eat it; this is my body.*

— Matthew 26:26

These passages demonstrate that as bread represents life and also represents Jesus, thus does Jesus (via bread) represent life. And because Jesus can also turn into bread, you can eat Jesus every Sunday and have life (via Jesus) inside you for eternity. This is known as transubstantiation.

Article II- Bread Pudding

No discussion of faith would be worthwhile did it not address the subject of the afterlife. Throughout history, this topic has engendered much speculation. Here I propose a new theory, derived from my cloistered contemplation of the following inquiry: what role does bread play in the Great Hereafter?

Bread inevitably grows old and stale, just as our bodies must wither with age. Yet though the spoilage of death may be certain, it need not be feared. For is it not true that, for the pure-of-bread, the Good Lord may transform our moldy loaves into bread pudding? What a treat!

Therefore, bread pudding (often referred to as simply "pudding") must be understood to represent both death *and* the afterlife. Indeed, while this theory has never before been formulated explicitly, the sentiment has nevertheless echoed through the ages:

> *They ran as swifte as a pudding would creepe.*
>
> - Armin, *A Nest of Ninnies* (1608)

One needs not know the context of this statement to apprehend that Armin is undoubtedly referencing the long, slow march of death.

And finally there's this little ditty from the Hibernians:

> *'Nerra thing but the big pudding. Why do you ax?*
>
> - Carelton, *The Pudding Bewitched* (1841)

Certainly, the text demonstrates that the Irish are a crude and savage people — a fact on which we can all agree. But they are also very pious. The preceding quote confirms that they are acutely aware of their own mortality.

Article III- Macaroni

The implications of this theory extend beyond merely solving the mysteries of life and death. Even those wise ancients could not have foreseen how complex civilization would become, and as such, their insights cannot begin to address the ways our relationship to bread has changed. How, then, can we account for these developments? The answer is as simple as it is obvious: macaroni.

At its most basic level, macaroni is but a different combination of flour and water. Derived from the Greek *makaroneia*, meaning "blessed dead," the word macaroni retains the spiritual implications of its alimentary antecedent while further offering us a host of fresh insights.

During the Renaissance, "modern man," as we know him now, was first conceived. Thus, it should come as no surprise that, since that time, the use of macaroni as a metonym for existence has grown steadily. Indeed, the municipal records for Palermo, Italy indicate that, by 1371, the price of macaroni had risen to three times that of bread. From this record, it is evident that modern life (macaroni), with all of its trappings — technological, artistic, economic, and otherwise — was at this point already considered three times as valuable as ancient life (bread).

The High Cost of Macaroni

The "price of macaroni" has continued to rise through to our present age, as documented in such works as a 1924 essay by F. Scott Fitzgerald called *The High Cost of Macaroni*. As I have not been able to locate the essay in question, I can only assume that it addresses the impact of inflation on the values of modern life.

The importance of macaroni has been recognized in more than just the musings of great thinkers, however; at one point, the pasta even inspired an eponymous social movement. The growth of this English society subculture is discussed in a 1770 issue of *The Oxford Magazine*. In describing the members of this group, which was comprised primarily of foppish, flamboyantly-dressed youth of the upper class, the magazine writes:

> *There is indeed a kind of animal lately started up among us. It is called a Macaroni. It talks without meaning, it smiles without pleasantry, it eats without appetite, it rides without exercise, it wenches without passion.*

For the Macaronis, it seems, modern life itself had such appeal that it even became their object of worship! As *The Oxford Magazine* astutely observes, the Macaronis, in embracing the material world with such ardor, also took on its worst qualities — apathy, ennui, cynicism, and wickedness. We can see this same principle at work in the modern use of the words 'bread' and 'dough' (not to mention 'cheddar,' discussed below) as synonyms for money. Even in our symbols, the Almighty Dollar has replaced the Almighty Lord.

Tragically, the Macaroni mindset appears to have won the day. Its descendants — the dandies and the hipsters — preserve its legacy of placing too much value on the trappings. What will this attitude cost us? What does macaroni portend for the future of faith?

Article IV- Macaroni & Cheese

As the foregoing discussion has definitively proven, in the modern era macaroni has come to represent Life, writ large. How, then, is a pious man of this age to bind this present conception of life with his own notion of the eternal afterlife? With cheese, of course.

Cheese, after all, is made of milk, a symbolic surrogate for the mother's milk which we all suckle, and thus a figure of our innate desire to return to the womb. As this is a condition that we all share, milk naturally serves as an emulsifier — it is, quite literally, the tie that binds.

Individually, each macaroni is but a solitary, isolated unit; add cheese, however, and we macaronis are no longer alone. We find salvation in our similarities, and our higher purpose is revealed. In Stevenson's *Treasure Island*, the marooned sailor Ben Gunn remarks, "Many's the long night I dreamed of cheese," a statement which, given the context, must allude to the fact that we as humans cannot exist in isolation. Only by associating with our fellow macaronis are we able to properly understand the meaning of life.

What else could possibly account for the fact that the most-eaten meal in America is macaroni and cheese? When we sit down to gaze long into that bowl of little yellow smiles, we are gazing back at ourselves. We are peering, indeed, into the universe in miniature.

Article V- Conclusion

On the unfolding continuum on which bread progresses to pudding, macaroni and cheese represents the final stage of evolution; because macaroni and cheese embodies a piquant new blend of apocatastasis (the return to our original form) and eschatology (the final disposition of our soul), it can have no direct pudding equivalent. To eat macaroni and cheese is to return our bodies to their original form — to have our sins forgiven, and our spirits purified. In so doing, we create a true heaven on Earth where no longer do we merely consume Jesus, but where we *become* Jesus! And if all be Jesus, surely it must be the case that He who revealed this fact (i.e., me) is God. Thus, I am God.

As God, I must conclude with a proverb.

You are what you eat,
The proof is in the Pudding.
- God

The High Cost of Macaroni

IT WAS MORNING when I was roused by the sound of sirens screaming toward the river. The rude awakening didn't bother me particularly; my slumber hadn't been particularly peaceful anyway. All night, my mind had been trying to digest *The History of Macaroni and Cheese* through a series of bizarre dreams. In one, the ramshackle ruins of Old Dutch City had been replaced with a series of historical structures, each built entirely of macaroni. Inevitably, countless gallons of fondue flowed between the banks of the Super-Sargasso River.

The monograph was clearly the work of a very learned, very disturbed, and very hungry man. But I will say this for Jones Very, Jr.: at least he wasn't afraid to tackle the big subjects.

I got up and went to return the holy text to its author. When I found him, he was sitting cross-legged on the ground. Oi was pacing around him in a circle — first clockwise, then counterclockwise — and seemed to be performing an incantation.

"You remember what to say, right?" said Oi softly.

Jones nodded.

"Don't forget, it's for this that the Prophet called you. And I'm his messenger."

"Yes, yes, I know," Jones replied.

"But you can't mention me to anyone. Because I don't exist."

"Of course. Of course."

"The Prophet will reward your sacrifice."

"God willing."

"Now go off and serve Him."

At Oi's command, Jones Very, Jr. rose slowly and brushed himself off. As he began to walk away, I attempted to hand him his manuscript.

"Would you like your writings back?" I asked.

Jones paused and looked at me with a sullen gaze.

"I need them no longer, my son," he replied cryptically. "Do with them what you must." With that, he began his plodding trek out of History Village.

As soon as Jones had disappeared from sight, I turned to Oi. "What the hell was that?" I demanded.

"Didn't he tell you? Turns out our faithful friend there stole the *Good Woman* last night and crashed her into a bridge."

"Hold on, what?"

"You should have seen me, Kip!" Oi exclaimed. "It was brilliant! I told him the Prophet foretold that his one true heir would reveal himself by claiming responsibility for a great disaster, then mentioned that, coincidentally, just such a disaster happened last night. I convinced him that by turning himself in, he'd finally get the recognition he deserved. And I promised him that for accepting whatever punishment he received, he'd be duly rewarded with everlasting pudding when he died."

"Is that all?" I replied. I was already sure it wasn't.

"I may have added that if he *didn't* confess, I'd turn his *face* into everlasting pudding."

I was appalled. Sure, it was naive for me to assume that we could just lay low until things blew over, hoping people would think the ship had become unmoored by a stiff wind or poor knotting or something. But at worst, I thought, we would be caught and have to take our lumps. I never expected that an innocent man would take the wrap.

"You can't believe that he should be locked up!" I argued. "He may be a little...eccentric, I'll admit, but he wasn't hurting anyone."

"Better him than me, man. I'm still on probation and there's no way in hell I'm going back to jail over a stupid boat. This way, we all win! We stay free and he gets to have a roof over his head, three squares a day, free meds — the whole nine! Way better than living in History Village if you ask me."

"But he didn't do it!"

"No, *Anselm*, you did! Are you really going to let a little joyride ruin your life? That looney would have ended up in the bin sooner or later anyway. All I did was help move the process along."

Oi had a point: if I were arrested, my otherwise unblemished record would be tarnished, my already meager bank account would be wiped out and, worst of all, I'd be stuck in Old Dutch City indefinitely. But I struggled to reconcile myself to his solution. Who's to say that Jones Very, Jr. didn't have fears of his own?

"Now since I did you a solid, I'm gonna need one in return," continued Oi, apparently satisfied that he had put the matter to rest. "Can you go down to the river and scope out the scene? Make sure everything's cool?"

"That's it?" I asked. "We're not going to discuss your little frame-up any further?"

"Nope. What's done is done. Besides, I have too much to do today to give it any more thought. So are you going to do what I asked, or what?"

"Fine."

"Oh, and if you see The Bust down there," he added, "remember to call him a big fat loser for me!"

The high cost of macaroni, indeed.

The Rummy Mummy

I ARRIVED JUST in time to watch a very solemn Jones Very, Jr. being thrown to the ground and placed in handcuffs. With a woeful glance, he tried to catch my eye; rather than engage, I bent over and pretended to tie my shoelaces, my shame compounding all the while.

I approached the knot of reporters and looky-loos that had formed, hoping to overhear something about Jones' confession, but their interest was barely roused by the arrest. They had come to watch the bulldozers raze what was left of Trinity Church. The *Good Woman* was already history, reduced to a pile of scrap wood and a couple tattered streamers.

Once Jones had been carted off to central booking, a man in a wheelchair rolled himself in front of the crowd to make an announcement. I could hardly believe my eyes: it was my old schoolmate, Anthony "The Bust" Van Eck! Like Oi, The Bust was someone I hadn't seen in over a decade, but those years had been far more generous to Oi. Where once The Bust had been svelte and handsome, he now was round and blubbery; where once he was spry and ambulatory, he now scooted around on two wheels. The rungs we occupied on the social ladder had been too far apart for us to have ever been close, but our interactions had always been cordial, if nothing else.

As The Bust prepared to begin, I heard someone shout, "Shut off those damn diggers! The Bust is going to say something!"

He winced; Anthony never had liked his nickname. The bulldozing continued.

"What a sad day," The Bust began. Even his voice seemed heavier: his timbre, once vague and shallow, was now deep and husky. "And on the very eve of the Quadricentennial celebration, no less! I thought it was only fitting that I should say a few words."

"You tell 'em, Bust!" yelled someone, for some reason.

"As we all can see, Trinity Church is no longer with us. She passed away this morning at the ripe old age of 165. In her long life, Trinity served as an elegant and enduring symbol of the city's ever-changing makeup. It will suffice to say that she will be sorely missed. Other than this small gathering, no official commemorations will be held, but the public is invited to stay and view the demolition."

Some people clapped. A few even cried. I did neither.

"Now, my fellow Old Dutchers," continued The Bust, "this tragedy forces us to make a crucial decision.

Are we going to sit idly by while drunken criminals hijack our respectable celebration and destroy the very symbols of our history? I, for one, am fed up. Fed up, I tell you! And so, on behalf of all that's good and right, I have decided, as the emcee and honorary King Tulip of the Quadricentennial, that I have no choice but to ban the sale and consumption of alcohol at all city events."

The Bust's proclamation did not go over well. At once, he was bombarded with jeers and expletives; someone even chucked a shoe at him. He evidently did not appreciate this abuse, because he promptly began to beat a hasty retreat from the scene. In the process, he rolled right over my foot.

The Bust recognized me as soon as he looked up to berate me for being in his way. "Well, well. Do my eyes deceive me? Has Anselm Kip returned to Old Dutch City? To what do we owe this pleasure?"

"Right now, you mean?" I wondered inanely. "Or, like, in general?"

"Both!"

"Well, you know, I didn't want to miss the Quadricentennial," I replied, deciding not to mention the encouragement I'd received from his archenemy, Oisin Fitzpatrick. "And when I heard about the church, I thought since I was here anyway I ought to pay my respects and stuff, you know?"

Lying was never my strong suit.

"Isn't it a shame?" cried The Bust, dropping his

head low as if in distress. "And let's not forget the ship, our *Good Woman*! One million dollars — sunk! Can you believe what this once great city has been reduced to? And I'll bet anything that your old pal, Oisin, had something to do with this travesty."

I swallowed hard. I didn't like the direction this discussion was heading.

"But at least it's given us a chance to catch up after all this time," I said, desperate to change the subject. "Tell me, how have you been, Bu— I mean, Anthony?"

"You can call me Bust, I don't mind," he responded resignedly; lying was never his strong suit, either. "I'll be honest, Anselm, things aren't great. Actually, they've been pretty crummy for a long time now. Ever since my father died, I have all these new responsibilities as landlord of his properties — my properties now, technically — and I'm just not up to it. Because of, you know, the incident."

"Yeah..." I answered, trying to conceal how awkward I was feeling. I hadn't even known that his father had passed.

"Not to mention, my sister's no help. Remember her?"

"Of course!" I replied, perhaps a little too eagerly. "The Pizza Princess!"

"Once upon a time, maybe. But honestly, there's hardly anything left to oversee anyway. Most of my buildings are empty. We even had to close the restaurant."

"Oh no! Not Trencherman's!" I exclaimed. I truly did lament the loss of the Van Eck's venerable eatery. Now where was I supposed to go for lunch?

"Well, as you can imagine, trying to make food without a sense of smell is something of a fool's errand," The Bust said, sniffling.

"So that never came back, huh?" I asked, trying to sound concerned. Really, I didn't care whether he could smell or not.

"It did not. And most of the time, the vertigo keeps me stuck in this chair. A dead nose and a dead body. Tell me, Anselm, is that any way to live?"

The Bust was obviously having a rough go of things, and I did feel sorry for the guy — but, boy, was he a bummer to talk to! I thought I'd try to lighten the mood by injecting some humor into our conversation.

"Well, you should look on the bright side, you know? At least when life takes a crap on you...umm...you can't smell it, right?"

The Bust scowled. So much for my attempt at levity.

"That's one way of seeing it, I suppose," he answered coldly.

Right then, the foreman of the demolition crew came running toward us. Behind him, the bulldozers were idling.

"Hey, Bust, we found something!" he shouted. "Come look!"

Anthony looked up at the foreman scornfully,

gestured at the debris-strewn field ahead of him, pointed at his chair, then looked back at the foreman with a huff.

"Oh, right. Sorry," said the foreman. "Anyway, whatever this thing is, it sure looks a hell of a lot like a body."

"Of course there would be bones!" replied The Bust, his impatience palpable. "You're digging underneath a church!"

"I didn't say we found no bones, Bust. This thing looks more like some kind of beef jerky."

The Bust sighed and turned back to me. "Anselm, go and have a look for me, would you?"

Relieved to be excused from the conversation, I climbed up the steps to the church with the foreman. As I scanned the rubble, I saw that the diggers had unearthed a series of large wooden cylinders, which were linked together by an elaborate network of ladders and piping; the body had been found inside the largest of these cylinders. Though the gnarled mass did indeed resemble an unappetizing slab of jerky, its features were undeniably human: a tuft of woolen hair, a tormented grimace, three crooked yellow teeth.

I was truly at a loss to explain this curio. When I came back to inform The Bust that I was as clueless as everyone else, he realized that an expert opinion would be needed and placed a call to Old Dutch University. A short while later, a frumpy little man with aquiline features arrived at the scene. He introduced himself as

Dr. Milo.

I escorted Dr. Milo back up to the church and accompanied him into the burial chamber. Dr. Milo proceeded to poke and prod the ghastly remains with a giddiness that was, to my eyes, more than a bit unseemly. When he had finished his cursory exam, he said, to no one in particular, "Yup, that's what I thought."

Before Dr. Milo could say more, the voice of The Bust reached us from the streets. "Well?" he hollered.

Dr. Milo and I climbed out of the hole. The scattered crowd that remained listened eagerly as he announced his findings.

"What we have found, underneath what remains of Trinity Church," he began, "are the vestiges of a 17th century rum distillery."

Some people oohed and aahed. A few even gasped. I did neither.

"To make rum, molasses is fermented with yeast and water, distilled, and aged. The wooden cylinders that the workmen uncovered are in fact the vats where that sweet, sweet drink was created. There are a number of historical references to the exquisite rum of Old Dutch City — and even of Shytt Bergie before that — but this is the first time any physical evidence has been found confirming that such an operation ever existed."

"But what about that...other thing?" The Bust asked.

"Oh, right. That." To Dr. Milo, the body seemed to be an afterthought. "I'm sure that's nothing more than the mummified remains of some dumb drunk — possibly a tipsy burgher, but more likely a transient or idiot — who fell into the vat and drowned long ago. The combination of sugary molasses and boggy peat is no doubt what preserved his body for the last four hundred years."

Fittingly, even this information ended up being distilled: the reporters on hand immediately dubbed the body "the Rummy Mummy."

To The Bust, this fortuitous discovery represented an opportunity: by adopting the Rummy Mummy as the official mascot of the Quadricentennial, he could gloss over the watery fate of the erstwhile *Good Woman*, into which he had sunk so much of the city's money.

"Dr. Milo, is the body in any condition to be moved?" he asked. He was practically licking his chops in anticipation.

"I don't see why not," the professor replied. "He's one sturdy bugger. Hell, if you strapped a handle on him, you could probably even carry him like a handbag."

"In that case, I hereby decree that these preserved remains of our historic forebear be taken at once to Patroon House! There, he will be properly groomed and attired so that he may serve as the Grand Marshal of the Quadricentennial parade!"

"With all due respect, Mr. Bust," interjected Dr. Milo. "I think this specimen should be taken to the university so that further research can be conducted."

"Nonsense! This poor soul shall be condemned to suffer a forgotten and ignominious fate no longer! Who better to remind us of the scourge of alcohol and vice that has plagued this city for centuries than our righteous forefather? I can think of no finer exemplar of temperance and decency than this Rummy Mummy!"

"Let the old drunk lie!" yelled someone. "Who are you to tell us not to drown ourselves in liquor if we want?" demanded another.

"Silence, turds! I'm taking the mummy for our celebration dammit!" he exclaimed. Then, apparently satisfied that the issue had been settled, The Bust turned to me.

I swallowed hard. I didn't like the direction this discussion was heading. "Anselm, I'm enlisting you as my aide-de-camp," he said. "Please grab the body and follow me."

A Long, Slow March

A QUICK WORD of advice: if you're ever asked to carry a mummy or bog person of any sort, politely demur. Then run headlong in the opposite direction.

The reasons for this can't really be appreciated until you've experienced them yourself. First, there's the smell. Personally, it reminded me of the time I barfed up a margarita on the floor of my grandmother's basement: because I did a such a shoddy job cleaning up the mess, the sweetly sour residue eventually blended with the basement's natural mustiness to create an olfactory nightmare that still lingers in my nostrils. Now, imagine that festering stink multiplied by four hundred, and you'll begin to have some idea what a rum-embalmed corpse smells like.

Next, you're going to actually have to touch the thing. I was surprised by how flat and dense it was, like some incredibly foul, fleshy pancake. Yet when I tried to pick it up, I discovered that other parts were — how best to describe them? — squishy. Any time I got a solid grip on the mummy's oddly smooth skin, I could feel his gelatinous innards sloshing around beneath my fingers.

Then, once you've got the body cradled in your arms, you won't be able to escape the hideous sight of it. The more you try to ignore it, to turn your head away and pretend you're carrying nothing but a particularly putrid piece of furniture, the more the gnarled carcass will seem to encroach on the corners of your vision. Those ghastly teeth! That goofy overbite! Just who did he think he was laughing at, anyway? Before long, you'll even start calling the corpse an asshole and accusing it of deserving its stupid death and the humiliation of going undiscovered for so long and the silly nickname that posterity has chosen for it and any other indignity you can think of. And your mind will start to ponder pointless questions: How much liquor had been filtered through the Rummy Mummy's tomb before being bottled and consumed? Did the distinctive flavor that Old Dutch Rum was famous for come from his pickled cadaver? Is he still laughing at me?

But the final trial will be enduring the attention that carrying carrion through the city during the busiest part of the day entails. Having to lug this freak for over a mile was bad enough, but because we took Big Street, the city's most prominent boulevard, I also had to contend with an endless stream of curious passersby who all felt the need to gawk or whistle or find some other way of being annoying. Some people even thought it would be fun to join us, swelling our entourage considerably. But did any of them offer to help? Would you? Not even The Bust, who was rolling along right beside me, who could have comfortably carried the mummy in his lap as he motored up the hill, showed any inclination to share my load. Instead, the only aid he offered was such unhelpful advice as *Watch your step, Anselm!* and *Be careful! You're about to drop him!* Thanks, your majesty.

For me, the only upside to this absurd march was that I was finally able to get a good look at Old Dutch for the first time in ages.

The city certainly had been gussied up in advance of the Quadricentennial, I had to admit. Every building, even the abandoned ones, had been lavished with a wealth of decorations. All along Big Street, and down every road branching off of it, I saw long vistas of variegated colors. Flags of every size, shape, texture, and hue fluttered from balconies, windows, and rooftops. Pendants and streamers dropped down from cornices and window casings; miles of garlands festooned the spires and turrets; and whole facades were covered with tasteful draperies, giving a vibrancy to the normally drab cityscape. Everywhere I looked, Old Cock and Balls was hanging proudly for all to see, and it seemed the whole city was plastered with shields, eagles, wreaths, and the vaguely ominous slogan, *ODC400...and counting!* Hundreds of tulips had been planted in every empty lot I passed, creating dozens of new gardens teeming with red, yellow, and orange petals.

Of course, I knew it was all just a temporary charade. Still, it *was* quite lovely.

At long last, we arrived at Patroon House, the sprawling estate where, for centuries, the Van Eck family has lorded it over Old Dutch City. When we reached the gates, The Bust, Mr. Mummy, and I found ourselves suddenly abandoned by our retinue, who knew full well that the doors to an exclusive residence such as this would never be opened to the likes of them. Not that I had ever had the status or connections required to secure an invite, either. I was just now being welcomed inside for the first time. To tell you the truth, the place kind of scared me.

I carried the mummy across the threshold as if we were a pair of newlyweds entering our honeymoon suite. It took me a minute to take it all in. Everything in the house — the impeccably appointed rooms, the imposing fireplaces, the antique gas lamps, the high-backed chairs, the massive oil paintings, the mounted heads of big game, even the entire wall of ancient leather-bound books — had a definite look-but-don't-touch feel about it.

I straightaway dumped the mummy onto the first couch I saw. Two old crones had been having tea nearby; upon being made acquainted with the new arrival, they quickly vanished.

"Right there is fine," said The Bust. "All we need

now is a sash, a cape, and a crown. I'm sure they can be found around here somewhere."

Meanwhile, that poor old drunk was sprawled out on the couch like Cleopatra. In life, he probably wouldn't even have been allowed to tie the Patroon's shoes; in death, he was his guest of honor. Well, don't let it go to your head, buddy.

"Anselm, would you mind helping me up the stairs?" The Bust asked.

I pretended not to hear him. I had wandered over to the bookshelf and now I quickly snatched a volume at random. It turned out to be *The Birds and Bridges of the Super-Sargasso Valley.*

> *The English sparrow was introduced to the environs of Old Dutch City in 1865. At the time, they were considered a great novelty and an even greater blessing. In neither respect are they regarded in the same light today.*

"Anselm, please!"

So that's how I ended up carrying my second lifeless body for the day. Up the stairs we went. Not one flight, mind you. Not two flights. But three full winding, narrow flights of stairs. Every few steps, The Bust's body would wobble and go limp, making the struggle of bearing the weight of his elephantine body particularly onerous.

"I really," he huffed, "really envy you, Anselm." Somehow, he was more out of breath than I was.

"Why's that?" I asked through clenched teeth. It

was taking every ounce of strength I had to keep gravity from jerking us back down the stairs.

"Because you had a chance to get out and took it," he replied. "And look at you now, living it up in California."

"It's not as glamorous as you think."

"I wish I had left too."

"Why don't you? Nothing's stopping you."

"Everything is stopping me! I can't go anywhere with all these responsibilities — which I never asked for or even wanted, by the way — and this never-ending list of things to do! Yet, for all that, I can't even get upstairs in my own house without taking the elevator or being carried! Look at me! Trapped by my obligations, and trapped by this stupid, useless body!"

With the end of our trek in sight, I realized that this probably wasn't the best time to ask why he hadn't proposed using the elevator in the first place. "Never pegged you for such a pessimist, Anthony," I said instead.

"Yeah, well, Old Dutch City has a way of bringing out the worst in people. It's a cancer that keeps growing and growing, eating away at you all the while. And for me, the tumor even has a name: Oisin Fitzpatrick."

The top of the stairs at last. I straightaway dumped The Bust onto the first couch I saw.

"Sorry for being such a downer, Anselm. It's just that I have no one else to talk to."

Rather than respond, I chose to catch my breath.

"Where are you staying while you're in town?" he continued.

"I'm not sure yet," I replied. I hadn't had the chance to secure any accommodations yet. So far, History Village seemed to be my only viable option. "You're more than welcome to stay with me if you'd like," offered The Bust. "We have a spare bedroom here. Actually, we have more spare bedrooms than I can count."

"Thank you, Anthony. I really appreciate it," I responded. I figured it would be a good idea to hedge my bets. I could always bail if a better offer came along.

"Well, I'm happy to have the company, of course, but..." he then added. Of course there was a but. Everything always had to be tit-for-tat around here. No one ever simply asked *How's life?* without having some ulterior motive. Couldn't we just exchange pleasantries and leave it at that?

He continued. "There is far too much to be done before the festivities begin tomorrow, and as you can see, I'm in no shape to do it alone. I think running a few errands for me in exchange for your room and board is a fair trade, don't you?"

"What did you have in mind?" I asked hesitantly.

"I just need someone to go around to all of my properties and check in on things."

He was being too vague for my liking. "How so?" I

wondered.

"Nothing major, of course. Just make sure everything's on the up-and-up, you know."

Nothing major, he says. Sounds like a suicide mission to me. The fear of being felled by a collapsing roof or shanked by a crackhead was one of my main reasons for fleeing this cesspool in the first place.

Nevertheless, despite the possible dangers, I replied with a cheerful "No problem!" Honestly, at that point I just wanted to get out of there and have a bit of time to myself.

"Wonderful! Just bring me that chair," he said, pointing to a spare wheelchair that was stationed nearby, apparently for just such an occasion. "And I'll go fetch you a list of addresses. By the way, your room is the second door on the right."

Not that I had any luggage to drop off, but I thought I'd take a peek at my quarters anyway. What I found might be described as a *Musée du Bust*. Trophies, ribbons, plaques, photos and news clippings were all on display, commemorating The Bust's brief but illustrious stint as a baseball player. Even his signed contract with the New York Mets had been framed and mounted. Unfortunately for The Bust, his professional dreams had been dashed before he ever made it to spring training.

Finally, no account of the collection would be complete without a description of its *pièce de résistance*: The Bust itself, a bronze sculpture of Anthony's adolescent head that was commissioned by his perhaps prematurely proud papa when the son was only fifteen. The likeness is quite striking, perfectly capturing the chiseled chin, Roman nose and broad jaw that Anthony was known for once. Of course, these days, if you really wanted to capture his profile, you'd be better off using a lump of dough.

Back then, The Bust's pa kept The Bust's bust on display on the counter at Trencherman's, ensuring that every customer and every employee — myself included — could worship at the altar of his golden child. But as you might imagine, narcissism on this scale aroused far more disdain than admiration, and before long it even earned its model a derisive nickname. Thus "The Bust" was born.

If the story had ended there, Anthony's high school moniker probably would have been forgotten by the time the city's 400th anniversary rolled around. But in the grand Old Dutch tradition of adding injury to insult, before Anthony could realize his ambitions, Oisin decided that what The Bust really needed was a particularly savage beating. In the condition Oi left him in, Anthony's hopes for a professional baseball career faded rapidly. Some called it a tragedy, but from that day forward his nickname took on a second, more pathetic meaning that he was never able to shake: forevermore, Anthony would be known as the talented kid whose erstwhile prospects for glory went bust.

Healing And Wellness

NATURALLY, THE BUST'S list of addresses spanned the entire city. Realizing that the ambiguity in his marching orders could be used to my advantage, I decided that I would do the bare minimum to fulfill his ill-defined request.

After all, "check in" could mean a lot of things — knocking on doors, collecting rent, confronting squatters, changing light bulbs, making chitchat — that all sounded terrible to me. But couldn't it also consist of merely sauntering past a handful of buildings, confirming their existence or non-existence, as the case may be, and moving on? So I opted to do that. And once I excluded the areas that I knew to be slums, crime-ridden, or both, the list narrowed considerably. In fact, I was left with only half a dozen addresses; conveniently, all were within a stone's throw of Patroon House.

The first place I came to was a small edifice whose storefront I recognized from my youth. Back then, it had housed a series of interchangeable hair-braiding salons. Now, according to a sign emblazoned with a mandala propped up in the window next to a bunch of planted herbs, it was home to the Old Dutch Healing and Wellness Center.

I could see no harm in checking in on what appeared to be a peaceful bastion of Eastern medicine, so I gave a quick knock and made my way inside. There, I was greeted by a sprightly — and quite pretty — young woman who was lying flat on her yoga mat, reposed in Savasana. A haze of incense lingered in the air, barely masking the unmistakable stench of cheap weed.

"Namaste!" the lady said, executing a series of bends and rolls until, suddenly, she was standing right in front of me. "How can I help you?"

"I'm not sure you can. Can you?"

"Of course I can!" she said with a smile as she furtively dislodged a wedgie. "We're the first, only, and very likely last healing and wellness center in Old Dutch City."

One was apparently more than enough. Looking around, I noticed that we were the only ones there. "Slow day?" I asked.

"Actually, now that you're here, we're having something of a busy day. If you're here for a session, I'm conducting a very special class today: Yoga for Halitosis."

Nothing about her statement made any sense to me, so I asked the only thing I could think of. "Is that meant to cure my bad breath or give me bad breath?" I wondered.

"Whichever you'd like. Any bad taste in your mouth will do." I weighed my options. On the one hand, I could hoof it around town for The Bust, which I didn't really want to do in the first place. On the other hand, I could kill some time with this lovely, limber, lonely young lass. Option 1: sore feet, bad vibes. Option 2: good breath, good vibes. It wasn't much of a decision.

"That sounds like exactly what I need. I'll take one Yoga for Halitosis, please."

"Terrific! Just have a seat on that mat over there, and we can get started, Mr. Kip."

"Wait, how do you know my name?"

"I remember you from before. I remember everyone."

"Well, what are the odds?"

"Old Dutch isn't that big of a place."

"True, very true."

"If you don't mind me asking," she asked, "what brings you back to your old stomping grounds?"

"Everyone's been asking me that. I guess you could say I needed a change of scenery."

"And you decided to come here of all places? Please don't tell me you're thinking about moving back!"

"God no!" I declared reflexively, without thinking, then added, "I mean, not that there's anything wrong with living here, of course. I just meant that—"

"No, I get it, but I'm not sure I buy your story. There must be something more to it. Hmmm." The way she was looking at me was making me feel funny. "Oh, I know! You must be going through a breakup! And you came here to, you know, clear your head, get some distance, and maybe, just maybe, gain a new perspective on your childhood, or something."

"Wow," I replied, genuinely impressed. "Good guess."

"Tell me about her."

"Do I have to?" I was feeling very ready to get started on Yoga for Halitosis.

"What does she do for a living?"

"Something incredibly boring that she never shut up about."

"Did you love her?"

"I thought so."

"Do you still love her?"

"It's possible."

"What is it that you love, or loved, about her?"

"At this point, I can't really remember."

"Perhaps you were confusing love and lust? It's very common. For guys, you know what love stands for, right? Lady Offering Vaginal Entry."

I chuckled. "Clever."

"Thanks! I came up with that one myself. Anyway, when was the last time you saw this lady?"

"A month or so ago," I replied, reflecting. "It's funny, I thought I had been dealing with things pretty well. Then, a couple weeks back, when I finally got around to doing some laundry, I found a pair of her stockings at the bottom of the hamper. It was a weird day all around. Earlier that morning, some dude chucked a bottle through my window. Shattered it to bits. So there I was, my window covered by a garbage bag flapping in the breeze like the flag of the world's saddest country, my floor still flecked with stray fragments of glass from two different sources, holding these stockings. The last reminder of warmth in an otherwise cold and empty apartment.

"I don't really understand why, but I walked into the bathroom with the stockings in my hand. Then, slowly, one leg at a time, I pulled them on. For a while I just stood there, checking myself out in the mirror; only when I heard the mail sliding through the slot in my door did I come to my senses. It was the letter inviting me back to Old Dutch City. And here we are."

"Yikes," she said, looking more than a little disturbed. "You're in worse shape than I thought. I'm going to need you to tell me more about your apartment."

"Of course," I replied. "Well, it's only one room, and it contains a bed, a couch, and two dying planets."

"Planets?"

"Did I say planets? Oh man, that's hilarious. I meant to say plants."

"Hmmm." She smiled at me inscrutably.

"And there's only the one window, which I've

already told you about. It looks out onto a filthy alleyway, and I don't actually know whether or not the window's been fixed yet. It wasn't when I left. I wrote my landlord about it, but he never answers my letters. It's too bad, too, because they contain some of my best writing. Do you think maybe he doesn't like my literary style? Perhaps he finds me too facetious, too ostentatious? Could that be why he also ignored my other letters, 'Curious Gas Smell' and 'Clogged Sink'?

"Anyway, to be honest, it's not the window that I'm worried about — it's the plants that really need the attention. For one thing, even when there is a window they never receive much sunlight. You see, the sun rises in the east and sets in the west, and my apartment faces north. So they're pretty much condemned to a life in the shadows — very sad, don't you think?

"Nevertheless, despite their chronically wilted appearance, they've somehow managed to outgrow their pots. Do you know how painful it is to see all their roots exposed, yearning for soil and light? And believe it or not, in San Francisco, dirt is surprisingly hard to come by. I mean, dirt*bags* they've got in spades, but I can't seem to find a single trowel's worth of good, 100% natural, all American *dirt*! What am I supposed to do, show up at the community garden near my place, measuring cup in hand, and ask, 'Hey brother, can you spare some dirt?' There's enough begging going on in that town already. At one point, I even considered sneaking in under the cover of night to filch a cup or two of their precious soil, but I figured that with my luck, that would be the one time a police cruiser was touring the neighborhood, and I'd wind up inspiring the headline, *Green-Thumbed Thief Busted Brown-Handed.*"

She giggled. She had a very charming laugh, I thought.

"Have I mentioned that I also have a cactus?" I continued, encouraged. "Although it's not much of one, to be honest. It probably wouldn't need any attention at all if I didn't have to dust it once in a while. The air in my apartment is very dry, so I get a lot of dust. I still can't figure out a good way to dust a cactus. Do you think I should ask my landlord?"

"I think you should probably cool it with the letters for a while."

"You're probably right," I replied.

"How long have you lived there?" she said, still surprisingly interested in hearing about my sorry excuse for a life.

"Ten years. Ten years in that same tiny room. You know, I've never lived that long anywhere else, not even back here. And you'll never believe how I ended up finding the place."

She actually looked intrigued. "Tell me," she said.

"It was a sign from above. I was *literally* struck by a sign from above. One night, I was out drinking at this bar, and I came out to smoke a cigarette. There were some people out front that I didn't want to talk to, so I walked over to this building down the street. And as I'm standing there, innocently polluting my lungs, a For Rent sign comes loose from the fire escape and smacks me right on the head."

"That sounds very painful."

"Oh, it was," I said, rubbing my scalp. "It actually feels pretty good unloading all this on you."

"Good, I'm glad. I think we're finally beginning to clear out all the bad breath you have trapped inside. Soon, we'll be able to replace it with new, good breath. But first, let's hang out in your apartment a little longer. Tell me, have you ever thought about dying there?"

"How do you mean? Have I ever speculated on the nature of death and its role in human existence while at that apartment? Or do I sometimes entertain the possibility that I could be at that apartment when my own life finally ceases? Either way, the answer is yes."

"Please elaborate."

"There are so many different ways I can see it happening. For instance, spontaneous human combustion is always a possibility — though honestly, it doesn't seem very likely. Or, since the ceilings are so high, maybe I could fall from a ladder while changing a light bulb. On the other hand, I don't actually own a ladder, so I'm probably safe on that one. Or I could slip and fall in the tub. I mean, I'm still young, so I doubt it, but you never know. But there could always be a fire, of course, and then I could die from smoke inhalation *or* from being consumed by the flames."

"Bleak."

"You're telling me! And I haven't even mentioned explosion from a gas leak, or asphyxiation from a gas leak, yet. And let's not forget home invasion turned deadly. Or choking. Or, I could have an undiagnosed heart condition or some other fatal affliction that could strike at any time. I could overdose on drugs unintentionally. Or intentionally. I could draw a warm bath and turn my veins inside out. Or I could turn on the gas and insert my head into the oven — it'd probably be the most use I ever got out of that oven, anyway."

"And how long do you think it would be before someone found you?"

"I don't know. Two, three weeks?"

"That's very troubling. But of course, confronting our mortality is difficult for us all, and I appreciate how open you're being. Now, let's move on to the clinical portion of the session. I'll ask you a few more questions, and your answers will help me identify the best way to heal your anguished heart. But remember, I'm not a doctor — though I did skim through a couple of old medical textbooks once."

"That's okay. I'm not picky."

"Have you ever had persistent sad, anxious, or 'empty' feelings?"

"Who hasn't?"

"Feelings of hopelessness or pessimism? Feelings of guilt, worthlessness, or helplessness?"

"Obviously."

"Irritability, restlessness?"

"Sounds like you've got me pegged."

"Loss of interest in activities or hobbies once considered pleasurable, including sex?"

"Everything except the sex part. Though to tell you the truth..."

"Fatigue? Decreased energy? Difficulty concentrating, remembering details, and making decisions?"

"All of the above."

"Thoughts of suicide or suicide attempts? Actually, I think we covered that already."

"Put me down as a yes anyway."

"Well, I think that about covers it. According to the people who decide what clinically depressed means, you are clinically depressed."

"No surprise there."

"Now I'm just going to ask you a few more questions to help me diagnose how close you are to a psychotic break. Hopefully, if we can recognize the symptoms ahead of time, we'll be able to prevent an irreversible brain fart."

"No brain farts. Got it." This girl seemed to be taking my answers seriously. It had been a long time since I had been listened to this attentively by anyone this attractive — or anyone else, really.

"First question. Do you daydream a lot or find yourself preoccupied with stories, fantasies, or ideas?"

"Quite a bit, actually."

"Great. Question two. Do you think other people call your interests unusual or say that you're eccentric?"

"All the time. Growing up here, it felt like there was a whole cottage industry devoted to it."

"Noted. Next question. Do familiar people or surroundings ever seem strange, confusing, unreal, alien, inhuman, or not part of the living world?"

"That's the only way they ever seem! Look at where I am right now. Is it supposed to seem real here?"

"Good point. Alright, last question, a two-parter. Have you ever felt that you might not actually exist, or do you ever worry that the world doesn't really exist?"

"Hmm. It's hard to say. Do you ever feel like that? That you don't exist?"

"Yeah, at times, I guess. On some levels."

"Exactly! I think of there being three worlds, each containing a different version of myself. There's the world as it is: I'm in it, but I'm powerless. Things happen, and I react. Let's call it the world without me. Here, I am whoever people say I am or want me to be. Then, there's the world through my own eyes. It's basically the same world, but now there's a tension between reactivity and proactivity. Here, I do have some control, but mostly only when I withdraw and try to look at it from the outside; I can project an image, but only hope it sticks. Finally, there's the world of my own making. Familiar people and places are here, of course, but there's also all this hocus pocus I've thrown in for good measure. It's all completely subjective: everything is what I say it is, everyone is who I say they are. Even the lies are true, at least to those, like me, who care to believe them. Even you, good hippie doctor, are just another character in this world, the world where I have complete control. But the ghosts are never far behind."

"Well," she said, "let's tackle those ghosts, shall we?" The girl was looking at me with a placid smile on her face, as though this kind of dialogue happened every day at the Old Dutch Healing and Wellness Center. "We'll start with a nice meditation. Sit back on your heels and focus your breath. Breathe in nice and deep, letting your belly fill with air. Hold it...hold it...okay, now exhale, slowly, from your mouth. Now repeat. We call this a cleansing breath — it gets all the lingering bits of existential halitosis out of your system. Now straighten your spine. Close your eyes, but not too tight. Just concentrate on the middle of your forehead. Stay comfortable, don't strain yourself. And remember to breathe. And smile! Always remember to smile, you sourpuss! Aren't you having fun?

"Okay, now we're going to open your brow chakra, also known as the 'third eye'. Keep focusing on that spot behind your forehead. Now, play an open B chord in your mind. Can't you hear it? Isn't that a nice, happy B chord? Let it ring out, then slowly fade. Now, repeat after me. Ommmm."

"Om," I said.

"Feel that tingle washing over you? That means the cleansing has begun. You're refreshing your mind and body. The plaque of your illusions is being rinsed away. We're awash in divinity now, sharing in the air of all creation. Now picture the color violet. Imagine a warm violet light enveloping you, radiating through you. Let it guide you. Follow its path. Now, tell me where it's brought you."

"I'm descending a bluff."

"Keep going. Where does the bluff lead?"

"I'm on a beach. The ocean is spreading out before me. There are steep cliffs, and little caves hidden between the rocks. The air is crisp. Far out to sea, there's a lingering tuft of fog."

"Have you been there before?"

"Yes."

"When? Were you with anyone?"

"Many times. With her."

"Is she there with you now?"

"No. Wait...there she is. She's combing the sand with her toes."

"Make her me. It's my toes combing the sand. What are you and I doing now?"

"Walking hand in hand. I twirl you around. We're laughing, dancing."

"How do you feel?"

"Happy. Content."

"Go deeper, Anselm. There's nowhere I won't follow you."

"We're in a cave. We've started a fire. You're suffused with light from two directions: a flickering yellow from the flames, and a soft white glow from the fog blanketing the ocean. The wind howls. Sparks leap from the fire and we trace their paths with our fingers intertwined. I brush the hair from your face. I kiss your cheek."

"Kiss me again."

"But you've turned away."

"Kiss me again."

"Now you've turned to dust and tossed yourself on the flames, smothering them. I pick up your ashes and put them in my pocket, so I can carry you forever. But when I look in my pocket, you're not there. Where have you gone, love? Come back to me, even if it's just for a little while. Don't make me spend another winter in this cave, shivering and alone. Come back to me, love. If only..."

At that moment, my concentration broke and I inadvertently opened my eyes. To my surprise, I discovered that we were now both naked, as if all that cosmic stardust melted the clothes clean off our bodies. Apparently, I had been lost so deep in the 'cave' that I had failed to notice when we both decided to disrobe.

Normally, I'd probably be more discreet and divulge few details of what happened next. In this case, though, the experience was so *sui generis* that I feel it must be documented for posterity.

In my eagerness, we exhausted the conventional positions rather quickly, and soon, at her suggestion, we graduated to more complex — and peculiar — contortions. First she introduced the Igloo, which involved high-arching back bends and a tray of ice cubes. From there, we transitioned to the Hayride, which was not unlike a wheelbarrow race, but required a lot more arm strength. Next was the 'Mordecai Three-Finger Brown,' in which a nine-inning baseball game was simulated in a most abstract (and filthy) way. If this is what the healing process required, I was happy to oblige. I can honestly say I've never had an experience that was more sensual — or more confounding.

"Feeling better?" she asked.

"Very much so, thanks."

"I suppose I'll see you at the parade this weekend?"

"That sounds great. I'll see you then."

Feeling extraordinarily at ease, I decided I had to leave, and fast, lest any spiritual gains I may have made be lost completely. I slunk away quietly while my hostess was repositioning the yoga mats. Before long I was venturing back down Big Street.

Trencherman's

NOW THAT I had come back down to Earth following my celestial excursion, I could no longer ignore the irresistible hunger growing within me. In particular, I found myself longing for the distinctive regional delicacies of Old Dutch City. Though I hadn't even thought of these dishes in years, my mouth now watered as I imagined polishing off a platter of Zippy Dogs (miniature hot dogs topped with meat sauce) and drowning myself in a bubbly Cheese Puddle (a sort of proletarian fondue). Or perhaps what would really hit the spot were some Riggies, maybe even a Neba or two. But what I truly wanted was all of the above! Though, naturally, I'd need to save enough room to have some Half Moons and Peppermint Pigs for dessert. What a treat!

Since time immemorial, whenever you were seized by a craving for any of these delights, the first and only place to go was Trencherman's, the beloved restaurant established and owned by the Van Eck family. Trencherman's was more than just a greasy spoon. For generations of Old Dutchers like myself, it was a rite of passage. It was a place of firsts — first jobs, first kisses, first heartbreaks, first heart burns; a place where late night revelries were held and early morning hangover cures were dispensed.

Their television ads played all day and night. Each one featured the incomparable Pizza Princess, played by none other than The Bust's little sister, Miriam Van Eck, forever eight years old because Papa Bust had only been willing to spring for commercials once. With a single wave of her magic wand, she would transform frowns into smiles and vegetables into hamburgers. Invariably, each spot ended with her affirming, with an adorable lisp, *Twechamen's is magicul!*

What had become of the Pizza Princess, I wondered. Certainly, The Bust didn't seem to think much of her now. Had she met her Prince of Pasta and noshed away into the sunset? Did she move to the suburbs to sell insurance to residents who still remembered her as royalty? Or was she still eight years old, still wearing a glittery dress?

Even though I had been told of its demise only hours ago, I walked to Trencherman's anyway, hoping against hope that The Bust (despite his inveterate humorlessness) had been playing a cruel joke on me earlier. Surely there had to be at least one part of my childhood that remained intact, didn't there?

Apparently not. The boarded-up windows and door papered with tattered notices were clear from a block away. I knew instantly that the once and future kingdom of the Pizza Princess was gone, lost in the plywood parade that marched up and down Big Street. There wasn't a single open business in sight.

I scratched Trencherman's off the list.

Cousin Pete

BY THIS POINT, I had dropped any pretense of completing the assignment The Bust had given me. Instead, I strolled idly along Big Street, willfully ignoring the police car that had begun to creep along behind me.

"Well, well, well," came the distorted voice from the loudspeaker.

Unsure of how to respond, I turned to find my cousin, Pete Kip, behind the wheel of the cruiser. A broad smile was plastered across his face.

Now that was a sight to see, I thought, chuckling. I knew Pete had joined the force, but this was my first time actually seeing him in uniform. Growing up, Pete's propensity for mischief was so second only to Oi's, but now, with a crew cut where his bleached blond spikes used to be and long johns covering his sleeve tattoos, Pete, it seemed, had become one of the good guys. I couldn't believe it, frankly.

Pete pulled up alongside me and stopped the car. Rolling down the side window and leaning over the passenger seat, he shouted to me, "You alright, man? You look like something crawled up your ass and died."

"Just looking for a place to eat," I replied, somewhat pathetically.

"What do you have a taste for? Zippies? Snappy Grillers?"

"At this point," I admitted, "anything."

"Hop in, stranger. I'll get you squared away."

I wasn't sure what was considered proper passenger etiquette for a police car. "The front or the back?" I asked.

Pete unlatched the passenger door and pushed it open. "The front, dipshit."

This was my first time inside of a police car — a miracle by any measure. It was a lot like I had pictured: the radio delivering crackly dispatches; the monitor flashing indecipherable codes; the metal cage that was the only thing separating good (the front seat) from bad (the back seat). And at my side, in charge of it all, was Pete.

"I didn't even know you were back in town," said Pete, as he causally weaved in and out of traffic. I buckled my seat belt. "But then, as I'm making my rounds, bored as shit, who should I randomly see bumming around but my cousin Anselm?"

"I meant to call," I replied. "This trip was kind of last minute."

"What, you ashamed of your family now?"

"Of course not, Pete. It's just that..."

"No time for me, but plenty of time for a loser like Oisin Fitzpatrick?"

I cringed. This was just what I needed: another test of my terrible lying skills — to a cop *and* a family member, no less.

"Oi?" I said, squirming in my seat. "I haven't seen Oi in ages."

"I see you're still a terrible liar."

"Okay. You're right," I replied, sheepishly. "I saw Oi last night...and this morning."

"And..."

"And...you know, we hung out a little."

Pete smacked me on the side of the head. "Wrong answer, stupid. This is where you're supposed to say, 'I'm in deep shit, Pete. Me and Oi stole a boat, crashed it into a bridge.'"

Fuck. Busted. I briefly wondered if it would be worth it to dive out of the speeding car to avoid further shame.

I stammered a response to deflect the inevitable shitstorm. "I thought you arrested someone for that."

Pete laughed. "Who? The Reverend Jones Very? We're just holding him for a psych eval. He'll fail with flying colors, I'm sure. Last I saw, he was preaching to the vending machines."

"I mean, sure, but couldn't he have..."

"Look, we have Oisin, on camera, stealing the boat. Done deal. As far as I can tell, you joined up later."

"How do you know?" I said, trying to defend the indefensible.

"I found your old fucking suitcase along the shore!"

Fuck. Double busted.

"At first, I thought it was just a coincidence, like maybe a bum pulled your bag from a dumpster or something. I mean, what kind of idiot leaves their shit at the scene of a crime? And that's when it hit me: my own fucking cousin's back in town and he didn't even call me."

Pete kept his eyes on the road the entire time he was dressing me down, but plowed through a yellow light anyway, forcing an old man with a cane back onto the sidewalk. I stared blankly at the inscrutable monitor screen, feeling both guilty and embarrassed.

"I'm sorry, Pete," I said at last. "I fucked up. I didn't know what Oi was up to, and the crash was an accident. I swear."

"It's a little late for that now, don't you think?"

"How bad is this? It'll blow over, right?"

"Fat chance. This is real bad, man. Millions-in-damages bad. Go-directly-to-jail bad."

"Is that where we're going? The slammer?"

"I should, but lucky for you, I'd rather eat lunch. Not to mention, I'm the only one who knows that Oi had an accomplice. Your suitcase is back at my place. If that goes away, this all goes away."

"But there's a catch, right?"

"Of course there's a catch, dummy. You've now made me an accomplice."

"Well, technically, you made yourself an accomplice by hiding my suitcase."

"I swear to fucking God, Anselm."

"Sorry, sorry. What do you want me to do?"

"Simple. Find Oisin and call me, but he can't know you're setting him up."

"But what if he rats me out?"

"Please. His word is dirt in this town. Less than dirt. No one will believe him."

We had arrived at the State House. Pete drove the cruiser into the main lot, pulled into a parking spot, and turned off the engine.

"I owe you big time for this, Pete," I said.

"Damn right you do. Just promise to knock this shit off, okay? What on Earth would even possess you to hang out with that guy?"

"I don't know. Oi used to be a lot of fun."

"Sure, Oisin always knew how to find drugs and booze and girls or whatever, but don't you think you're getting a little old for that shit? And let's not forget that Oisin spent three years in county jail for putting The Bust in a coma. And for what? Twenty bucks! Twenty bucks, and he beat The Bust to a pulp. Cost him his contract with the Mets too! Now the poor kid just sits around like a fat tub all day. If you ask me, that's the real reason his dad dropped dead: a broken heart. I mean, shit, man, The Bust had talent. Real 'Welcome to

Old Dutch City, Home of Rookie of the Year Anthony Van Eck' talent.

"And on top of all that, you think Oisin ever learned his lesson? Of course not! As soon as he gets out of jail, he's right back to the same old shit. One day, we'll catch him selling weed. Another, shoplifting. Another, getting drunk and smashing up a bar. It never ends."

"If he's that bad, then why isn't he back behind bars?"

"He's a slippery fucker. Jumps bail. Files bogus petitions — he fancies himself a jailhouse lawyer now, if you haven't heard. Works the system then goes into hiding, every fucking time."

As I sat with Pete in his car, thinking to myself, the State House clock chimed the hour. "Shit! I lost track of time," he said. "All this talking and now I'm late for my detail. Rain check on lunch?"

"That's fine," I said, though my stomach felt otherwise.

"And seriously, call me the second you find Oisin. Do that and all this goes away."

"Thanks, Pete," I said as I got out of the car.

"No sweat, man. That's what family's for."

Remembering The Scrunchie
(and other, more relevant, matters)

ONCE PETE HAD disappeared into the State House, where he was presumably going to be dragging prisoners before judges all day, I turned my attention to the urgent matter of food. I walked across the street, where there was a somewhat respectable-looking ATM machine, then hustled over to the hot dog stand nearby. In the moments before my arrival, I watched as the proprietor dislodged no fewer than three boogers from his nose and consumed them; nevertheless, I ordered three Zippy Dogs with the works. The stomach wants what the stomach wants.

Too hungry to bother going anywhere else, I stood beside the cart while I made short work of my meal. Between bites, I gazed up at the State House. The structure — a massive gray limestone tower with arrow-slit windows and a steep gabled roof — was as imposing as I remembered, like a medieval abattoir.

Along with Patroon House, the State House was one of only two buildings in the city left from the

Dutch era, and it has served as the backdrop for many great moments in Old Dutch history: here, the Dutch formally ceded Schytt Bergie to the British; here, Tory prisoners were held during the Revolutionary War; on its steps, the Declaration of Independence was read; through its arches, Lincoln's coffin was carried. The State House also holds the distinction of being, during a third grade field trip, the first place I ever peed my pants. Twenty-odd years later, Zippies racing through me, I was convinced it would become the first place I pooped my pants, too.

As I scanned the area in search of a bathroom, who should I suddenly spot racing out of the State House but Oisin, wearing a crumpled suit and carrying a battered briefcase. Somehow, despite the fact that he was currently the most wanted man in Old Dutch, Oi had managed to slip in and out of the most official building in the city, apparently unscathed.

I ducked behind the hot dog stand and let Oi pass. I watched as he hurried across the plaza in front of the State House, his scuffed loafers trampling over every newly-planted tulip in his path. Then I set out after him, being sure to maintain a buffer of several bodies between us so I wouldn't be spotted.

While working to stay hidden, I recalled that this wasn't the first time I had pursued someone surreptitiously. During the summer of my fifteenth year, shortly after I first started working at Trencherman's, I became briefly but woefully besotted with a co-worker of mine named Emily Tromp. She wore bright, shiny braces and smelled of hairspray, and from what I could tell there wasn't an inch of her that wasn't covered in freckles.

As romantically inept as I am today, I was cripplingly more so back then; you might say I had a head full of poetry and a mouth full of cotton. Naturally, this precluded the possibility of any meaningful conversation between us. Hoping to break this impasse, I ultimately decided the best solution would be to follow her after she left work. To, you know, get to know her or something, I guess.

Sadly, her evening strolls yielded little insight. Every night, without fail, she went straight from Trencherman's to the gas station where her father worked, grabbed some magazines from the rack, and sat behind the counter reading them. Occasionally, she would help to unpack a box or two. Needless to say, the spectacle wasn't exactly thrilling.

I kept this up for a full two weeks. In that time, I came no closer to uncovering some secret that could help me spark her interest, or at least be used to inspire the necking and amateur intercourse I so viscerally longed for. Finally, as my yearning grew increasingly unbearable, this sad and misguided affair reached its fateful conclusion.

I was out on the prowl once again, my head crowded with a jumble of thoughts both innocent and obscene, when I saw something fall from her pocket.

Unaware that she had dropped anything, Emily continued walking. Seeing an opportunity (to do what, I'm not sure), I stealthily scurried over to discover what she had left behind. It was a scrunchie! I hastily snatched it up and, for reasons still unknown to me, shoved it down my pants. To my adolescent mind, it felt as though a breakthrough had been reached: something of hers was now intimately acquainted with my erection.

Unfortunately, the illicit rush I was feeling was short-lived. As soon as Emily had disappeared from sight, I saw myself as the fool I was: a fifteen-year-old boy with a cheap scrunchie around his dick. Overcome with shame, I chided myself for being such a creep, dug the scrunchie out of my pants, and threw it in the trash. After that, I left Emily alone, convinced that if we ever did speak, my guilt would inevitably reveal itself.

Years later, I discovered that Emily and I had followed similar paths through life. Like me, she had moved away, gone to school, even published some writing. When I read about this, I wondered if perhaps we actually had been soul mates after all. Unfortunately, since it was from her obituary that I learned these facts, it was useless to speculate. She had been hit by a bus while on her honeymoon in Buenos Aires. Poor Emily.

Of course, none of this was germane to my pursuit of Oisin, though I did keep expecting to see a scrunchie fall from his pocket, or to discover that he had been leading me to a gas station all along. Alas, this was not to be. Instead, I found that I had returned, much earlier than expected, to Patroon House.

As Oi entered the gates, I hid behind a car parked across the street and watched the curious scene unfold.

"Hey, dummy!" Oi yelled at the house. "You didn't know it Bust, but I've had a secret weapon this whole time! I've finally bested you, once and for all, and there's nothing you can do about it!" Then he simply sauntered away, leaving the briefcase by the door.

Now I was faced with two options: I could keep tailing Oi as he proceeded to whatever item was next on his absurd agenda, or I could find out what was in the briefcase and whether this recent development made any more sense to The Bust than it did to me. Still feeling the Zippies more urgently than ever, I chose the latter.

As soon as the coast was clear, I walked up to Patroon House and began to rap on the door. "Who's there?" The Bust asked cautiously. Then, in response to my incessant knocking, he added, "Go away!"

"Which is it?" I replied. "Do you want to know who it is, or do you want me to go away?"

"Anselm? Is that you?"

"Of course it's me. Who else would I be?"

"Is *he* with you?"

"He who? Oi? No, he left."

"Are you sure?"

"He's not here, okay! Just let me in! If I don't get to

a toilet soon, you're going to have a huge mess on your porch!"

Finally, The Bust opened the door. "Down the hall, second door on the left," he said in a shaky voice. He was clutching a fireplace poker, and it was obvious he had been crying. When I returned a few minutes later, I found The Bust in the fetal position on the sofa.

"Why won't he just leave me alone?" he cried. "I'm so sick of it, Anselm!" After that, he broke down completely.

"He seems to think there's some great rivalry between us, but there's not! I don't care what he does, I never have!"

"Have you tried talking to him?" I asked. "You know, hash things out, come to some sort of truce?" Knowing Oi, I was sure such a gesture would be futile, but I didn't know what else to say. All these tears were making me uncomfortable.

"What good would it do? For years his only goal was to ruin my life. And why? Because I gave him a job at Trencherman's once? That was a million years ago. He was living on the street, what was I supposed to do? But was he grateful? Nope! He stole from the register, right under my nose! And when I tell him to knock it off, he attacks me! I know he blames me because he wound up in jail, but that was all him."

"I know, Anthony. What happened to you was terrible, and it's cost you a lot. But, like you said, that was a long time ago. At some point, one of you has to be the bigger man and move on, and we both know it's not going to be Oi. Otherwise, this could go on forever."

"Don't you think I realize that? But what am I supposed to do? I can't escape him! Now he's even harassing me at my doorstep, yelling who knows what about a secret weapon and him winning something. I don't know what the hell he's talking about. I don't have anything left to lose!" The Bust trembled as he spoke. He probably hadn't been this worked up in years.

"He left this briefcase outside," I said, gesturing to the spot by the door where I had set it. "Do you want to open it?"

"What if there's a bomb in there?"

"That's insane. Why would he leave a bomb at your door?"

"Why wouldn't he — he's insane! And he said he had a secret weapon, right?"

"I don't think he meant it literally. Besides, it's not much of a secret if he's yelling about it in the streets."

"I'm going to call the police."

"It's not a bomb, Anthony!"

"How do you know? Are you a bomb expert?"

"Wouldn't we hear ticking or see some wires or something?"

"They don't make bombs like that anymore."

"Oh, so now *you're* the bomb expert."

"I think it's a fair point."

"Look, I'm going to open it. If we're blown to bits, I apologize in advance."

The Bust covered himself in pillows while I unlatched the briefcase. There was no explosion when I opened it, only a bundle of papers. I removed the sheet on top of the stack and read it aloud.

"Upon reviewing Petitioner's motion for adverse possession, this court finds that Oisin Fitzpatrick has been proven to be in open, notorious, and continuous possession of the real properties described in Exhibit A (hereinafter, the "Properties"). As such, Petitioner's motion is hereby granted, and all right, title, and interest in and to the Properties shall be transferred to Mr. Fitzpatrick forthwith, without prejudice or delay."

I quickly flipped through the rest of the papers until I found Exhibit A. Other than a few notable omissions (the Healing and Wellness Center, for example), the list was identical to the one The Bust had given me earlier.

"I have no idea what any of that means," The Bust admitted.

"I don't either," I admitted. "But if I were to guess, I think Oi invoked squatter's rights. Apparently, he stayed in all these vacant buildings long enough so that he now owns them all."

"And the court allowed this?"

"I guess so."

"So, let me get this straight. I don't own any of

those buildings anymore? Oisin does?" The Bust's voice had begun to tremble once again. "That's right," I replied, bracing myself for another meltdown.

"Yippee!" he exclaimed, ridiculously. "I'm free! If Oisin wants all those crummy old properties, he can have them! Hell, let him have this whole miserable city for all I care!"

I was confused. "You're not...upset by this?" I asked.

Then I heard something I had never expected to hear: The Bust laughed. "Why would I be upset?" he wondered. "Those dumps were the only thing keeping me here. Such a burden, such a hassle! They were constantly getting vandalized, broken into, falling down. I mean, you saw all of them today, right?"

"Yeah," I lied. "All of them."

"Good riddance!"

His jubilation was still hard for me to grasp. "But, what about, you know, your family's legacy? They founded this town."

"What legacy? The legacy of my dead father, who turned his children into mascots? My mother who ran off? My hippie sister who wants nothing to do with me? Some legacy. My family got here first, that's it. Are we really any different from Oisin? Isn't the whole Van Eck empire built on squatter's rights?"

"I'm...really surprised to hear that. I had no idea you felt that way."

"Getting out of this town has always been my goal,

Anselm, and Oisin is the only reason I didn't take off a long time ago. He may have spent a few years in prison for what he did to me, but how does that compare to the prison he's trapped me in? I bet he's out there right now, gloating, thinking that he's finally scored the ultimate humiliation. But the truth is, he's set me free."

"Any idea where you'll go?" I inquired.

"I don't know. Where's the exact opposite of here? That's where I want to go. A place without history. A place where no one ever had to look at a statue of my head while eating a plate of chicken riggies. A place where there's no Oisin Fitzpatrick. And I'm not going to wait another day, either. I'm going straight to the airport."

Was he really going to leave before the Quadricentennial? "But what about the parade?" I asked.

"Fuck the parade!" said The Bust. Buoyed by his newfound sense of freedom, The Bust rose from the sofa and pushed his wheelchair aside. "And fuck Old Dutch City!" he said, turning back to me as he walked toward the door, "Anselm, would you do me one more favor?"

"Sure, I guess. What is it?"

"If you see Oisin, I want you to give him a message for me. Tell him The Bust says thanks."

The Rummy Mummy 2:
The Conversation

THAT NIGHT, DESPITE my exhaustion, I couldn't sleep. The twin bed in The Bust's old room was much smaller than I was used to, and the sheets were so rough that I decided they must have contributed to his long-brewing resentment toward his family. Even tossing and turning was too uncomfortable, so I simply lay stiff and motionless, listening to the clock tick off second after second with nothing to break up the monotony but the chime announcing the arrival of each new hour. It was late (or early, depending on your perspective). An uneasy calm had settled over the house, but though The Bust was gone I wasn't entirely sure it was empty. Hadn't there been a couple of old ladies here earlier? In any event, I felt like I was trapped inside some ancient tomb, and now it was too late to find other accommodations.

Finally, I decided to get up. I left my room and began stalking the halls, eliciting unsettling groans from the floorboards with every step. Gas lamps cast ominous shadows across the portraits of long-dead Van Ecks; their hollow stares seemed to follow me everywhere, making me feel most unwelcome, like an intruder in their home.

As I passed through the halls of the third floor and made my way down to the second, then the first, I tested out every couch and chair I came across, but everywhere the prospect of sleep seemed equally remote. Eventually, my options dwindling, I descended into the cellar, a dank and chilly chamber enclosed by the building's stone foundation. The place was seriously spooky — I half-expected to see skeletons chained to the wall.

The darkness of the room was nearly impenetrable; however, as my eyes adjusted, I noticed the faint glow of what appeared to be a candle burning in the distance. Taking short, cautious steps, I approached it. Slowly, the light grew brighter, until the outline of a man was revealed. Judging from his silhouette — the tightly-cropped Van Dyke beard, the frilly ruff collar, the sugar loaf hat — he could have stepped straight out of a Frans Hals painting. Was this a man, or just the remarkable likeness of one, I wondered. But while his presence was startling, I admit, mostly I just felt underdressed.

"Master Bust, is that you?" the man asked, his voice heavily accented.

When he spoke, I was taken aback. Master Bust? If this was one of the house servants, it appeared that

Anthony had insisted on a very peculiar dress code.

"Nope, it's just me. Anselm."

"Oh, Mr. Kip! What a treat! How kind of you to come and join me!"

As I drew near, I caught a whiff of the man. He smelled like a compost heap, but something about his rank odor seemed familiar.

"I must thank you from the bottom of my heart for your forbearance this morning."

"How do you mean?" I asked, truly puzzled.

"Why, surely it must have been trying to carry me up that hill."

"I'm sorry? I still don't follow."

"Oh, dear. My good man, it is I who should be apologizing. I suppose a proper introduction is in order. My name is Jan, though you may know me better by the crude appellation with which I've been associated of late: the Rummy Mummy."

"Bullshit!" I exclaimed, justifiably for once.

"As unlikely as my claim may seem, I jest not," he replied.

"Alright," I said, curious to see how far he was willing to take this 'jest'. "Prove it."

"To prove or disprove one's own existence is the province of philosophers, which, alas, I am not, any more than you are. Is not my very presence before you confirmation enough?"

"I'm not saying you don't exist. I just don't buy that you are who you say you are."

"I do not intend to enter a debate with you over my identity. Should you not wish to engage in conversation, you may go back upstairs if you choose. But consider this: when is it you saw me last?"

"Well, if by you, you mean the desiccated corpse discovered underneath Trinity Church, well, then, a couple hours ago, when I tossed 'you' on the sofa in the living room."

"Do you recall seeing me when you were there last?"

I didn't. Actually, I was pretty sure I had tried to sleep on that same couch as I made my rounds through the house, but I didn't have the energy to go back and check. "Let's say, for the sake of argument, I accept that you really are the Rummy Mummy. Does that mean you're here as a ghost?"

"Not necessarily."

"Hallucination?"

"To some degree, perhaps, but not entirely."

"Demon?"

"Heavens, no!"

"So you're human?"

"So it would appear. But as you know, appearances can be deceiving. Perhaps you should think of me as...an essence. That's it, an essence. Let's go with that."

"That doesn't really clear anything up. Are you alive, or are you dead?"

"What a silly question, Mr. Kip! I'm dead, of course, therefore I cannot be alive. On the other hand,

I'm alive and speaking to you, therefore I cannot be dead."

"Right. Whatever you say."

"But, oh my, where are my manners? Can I offer you something to eat?"

"What do you have?" I asked. I didn't see or smell anything that I would consider edible.

"I have prepared a true delicacy, a delicious pudding of macaroni and cheese."

"Huh. So is it true, that macaroni and cheese holds a special significance to the afterlife?"

Even the Mummy seemed confused by the question. "No, I'm afraid it does not," he replied.

"Well, as a denizen of the afterlife, would you be interested in a book whose central theme was built around that premise?"

"I find the prospect incredibly unlikely."

"Figures. Anyway, I'll pass on the pudding. I had some Zippies already."

"Very well. More for me, as they say in your era," he said. He did not, however, stir, and there remained no sign of the savory dish he had offered.

Still, perhaps this anachronistic apparition could shed light on some other perplexing matters, I thought. Besides, I didn't want to let the conversation lag. In this creepy context, an awkward silence would have been too much to take. So, deciding to make the most of the situation, I began, "Can I ask you a question, Mr. Mummy?"

"Of course! What purpose would conversation hold if you could not? But please, call me Jan."

"Does it sadden you that it took so long for your body to be discovered?"

"For many years, it did. But, eventually, I came to accept that no one was looking, or knew how to find me, and that it was unlikely I would ever be found. So to be discovered at long last — what an unexpected gift! Yet has it not always been the fate of many not to be appreciated in their own times? Are we not told that patience is a virtue? And behold, has not my own virtuous patience been justly rewarded with fame? In my judgment, such compensation is more than fair. Today I dine at Patroon House! In my day, such would have been unthinkable."

"I know the feeling," I replied. "But what have you been doing all this time?"

"Lying about, mostly. There wasn't much else to do, especially once they built a church on top of me. It was particularly trying on Sundays. The singing, the sermons, the tolling of the bells: after two centuries of unadulterated silence, the sounds of salvation brought me nothing but misery."

"So tell me. What was Old Dutch City like in your day?"

"As a lifelong resident of Schutt Bergie, I have few insights to share concerning your Old Dutch City. But, when I did walk the streets of this burg, it was indeed splendid! There was many a tavern to frequent, and many a loose woman to frequent, too. By night, my confederates and I would spend small fortunes on rum while we devised endless schemes for realizing even greater fortunes! It brings me such joy to remember those days! If a place be but what one makes of it, then never has there been a place such as Schytt Bergie!"

I wished the Schytt Bergie of today inspired the same enthusiasm in me. I wondered if this strange specter had any thoughts about what his once beloved colony had been reduced to. "As you may know, we're celebrating the Quadricentennial of the city...well, today, actually, and they're making a lot of hoopla about it. How do you feel about that?" I asked. "I mean, it's not like anyone seems to care about what actually happened."

"Don't be so dour, Mr. Kip! It's just a bit of harmless fun. Who doesn't find that the flattering mists of time make the past more pleasant to look upon? Posterity is founded upon repetition, not veracity, after all. Should details be changed or facts omitted, it is only because the story proves better without them."

"But how are we supposed to remember what happened if we never know what happened in the first place?"

"Perhaps not everything is worth remembering, Mr. Kip."

I didn't know what to say. At this point, I was feeling pretty bummed: I was debating an entity that almost certainly didn't exist, and I seemed to be losing.

"I'll be honest, Jan," I said. "I'm beginning to regret this whole trip. I think my reasons for coming back were...not good ones. I feel like there's no one I really want to see, and nothing I really want to do, so instead I'm just bouncing from one thing to the next without any sort of plan or goal. Does that make sense? Do you think it was a bad idea for me to come back?"

"Do you think it was a bad idea for me to drunkenly stumble into a vat of rum and drown? It happened. Somehow, those decisions lead both of us here. So it goes."

"Thanks, I guess. But I was really hoping for a bit more guidance."

"Mr. Kip, the only advice I can give you is that which I always gave myself when facing consternation of the sort that afflicts you now," the 17th century spirit replied. "Get thee to a brewery!"

Tempus Fugit

WHILE MY CONVERSATION with the Mummy wasn't the most spiritual experience I had had that day, it did leave me in a rather metaphysical mood — so I was happy to heed his advice and repair to the nearest watering hole. Once I left Patroon House and got my bearings, I realized that I was only a few blocks from the Tempus Fugit Saloon (also known, in local parlance, as the *Tempus Fuck-It*). While it wasn't the oldest, or nicest, or cleanest tavern in the city, the Fuck-It was certainly the cheapest.

It had been many years since my first trip to this particular pub. Due to its lax (i.e., nonexistent) ID policy, I was only 17 at the time. Most nights, I could be found among the throngs of underclassmen who packed the place, getting snookered on twenty-five cent drafts. In addition to weak drinks, the Tempus was always well-stocked with underage girls, so much so that it was widely rumored that the owner, a grumpy sot named Liam Touhey, had a taste for teens. In all the time I spent there, however, I saw nothing to suggest that Touhey's motivations were anything other than pecuniary.

Overall, my run at the Tempus was a good one. However, like most of its patrons, I eagerly graduated to more mature establishments upon reaching the age of majority. Once you've become the oldest guy at the bar, drinking with amateurs rapidly loses its appeal.

Now, years removed from those halcyon days, I passed through the threshold of the Tempus Fugit once more. Greeted by the same familiar mainstays of my youth — the smell of bleach, the broken pinball machine, the disapproving expression on the face of Liam Touhey — I immediately felt right at home. The only thing missing, curiously, was the ever-changing crowd of teens that usually reached its most raucous at this time of year.

As I entered, Touhey kept his eyes fixed on the TV above the bar. Given the desolation of the place, you'd think he'd be excited to have a customer of any sort, but I can't say I was surprised by his indifference. I took a seat at the bar. "Long time, no see, Touhey," I said.

"Miss me?" he replied, still focused on the late-night sports recap filling the screen.

"Not at all," I admitted.

"Good," he said, finally turning to look at me, though his expression remained as blank as ever. "This place is for forgetting the past, not getting all sappy about it."

"Still serving watered-down booze to the criminally underage?"

"Yep. Not that you got anything to worry about these days, by the looks of you. Way I see it, kids are gonna drink, and they've gotta spend their allowances somewhere, so why not here? Hell, it's not like there's anything else for them to do around here. And as long as the right palms are greased, who's gonna give a fuck, anyway? Shit, if I threw an extra fifty a week to the alderman, I could probably open a day care center in this place."

"God bless you, Touhey. I'll leave you my rotten liver when I die."

"Save it for someone who gives a shit," he replied. Then, a look of recognition finally crossed his face. "Wait, I remember you. You're Pete's cousin, right? Anton or Andrew? I'm shitty with names."

"That's right. Anselm Kip."

"Hey, was that you I saw carrying the mummy today?" he asked. "You an undertaker now or something?"

"I wish. Transporting corpses is just a hobby."

"Good for you. Now you gonna order something, or are you just planning to chew my ear off all night?"

"Sure," I said, as I took another look around the bar. In my day, it had never been as dead as it was right now. "I'll have a beer. I guess you ought to make at least one sale tonight."

"Thanks bub. Since they banned booze during the

Quadricentennial, I guess everyone decided to stay home and bone their old ladies sober for a change. It's been like a tomb in here all day. But, on the plus side, if no booze means no Oisin Fitzpatrick, then hallelujah!"

Now, the Devil may not appear every single time you speak of him, but it was only fitting that Oisin should come waltzing in. Wearing a chintzy paper crown and brandishing a kazoo, which he used to announce his presence by tooting a short but festive reveille, Oi looked as though he had just raided the party favors from a child's birthday.

"Lock the doors and drop your drawers, King Saturn has arrived!" Oisin announced to no one in particular. Then, noticing me standing at the bar, he said, "Oh, hey, Kip. How's it going? What are you doing here?"

"Drinking," I replied.

"Very good. As you were."

In all the times I had watched Touhey interact with drunken patrons, I had never seen him lose his temper. Now, as he dealt with Oi, I could practically see steam coming from his ears.

"It would be wise of you to get the fuck out, Oisin," he said. "You're not welcome here."

"What for, Touhey?"

"Where the fuck to begin? Pissing in my sink, for one. Fucking up the pool table. Mouthing off to patrons. Stiffing me on your tab. Take your pick."

"Tsk, tsk. That's no way to talk to your new

landlord, Touhey. Oh, I guess you haven't heard. After all, the news is still piping hot off the press. In a landmark decision sure to go down as one of the most important in legal history, the Superior Court of Old Dutch City has awarded me ownership of The Bust's properties, including this garbage heap."

"Bull. Shit," he replied. Then, turning to me, he asked, "Anselm, have you heard anything about this?"

"It's true. More or less," I replied. "I think there's a few places he didn't get."

"Damn right it's true!" Oi yelled.

"True or not," Touhey seethed, "I'll cut off my sack before you see a dime in rent from me!"

"In that case, I suppose you'll have to get used to tending bar *il castrato,* my friend. But you'll find that I'm a far more munificent landlord than your previous *rentier,* that's for sure. And to ensure your till stays full, I've invited a host of scamps, wags, wastrels and merrymakers to come here and celebrate the Quadricentennial by getting blasted on your potent potations. They'll be arriving any minute now."

Touhey was unmoved. "The bar closes in an hour, crowd or no crowd."

Oi affected a look of blind confidence and blithe indifference as we waited. And waited. And waited, but the promised multitudes never came barreling through the doors. After a while, Touhey, who had started watching an old Western out of boredom, began dozing off. Oi paced around, rehearsing what sounded like some sort of demented limerick:

> *Let us bend over statues and peek under their robes;*
>
> *Let us goose politicians, wave dough under their nose;*
>
> *Let us cheat all the cheats and fill our pockets with gold;*
>
> *And let us smell the hair of angels 'til we grow old!*

Every once in a while, Touhey would yawn loud enough for Oi to hear. For my part, I chose to amuse myself by watching to see if they'd be able to ignore each other this intently for the entire hour. Finally, Oi's time was up. Not a single person had arrived.

"Some party," said Touhey with undisguised contempt. "You've really outdone yourself this time."

"Wait. Just give me a few more minutes," Oi pleaded.

"Bar closes at four. It's the law."

"Since when have you given a fuck about the law?" replied Oi indignantly.

"I'm the law around here and I'm tired. You and your imaginary friends can go party elsewhere." Then Touhey walked over to the window and began switching off the neon signs.

"Turn that sign back on!" Oi screamed. "I order you!"

"Go fuck yourself," Touhey replied. As he returned to the bar, Touhey casually snatched the crown off Oi's head, crumpled it up, and tossed it in the trash.

"So that's how you wanna play this?" Oi fumed, his face disfigured by fury. He reached for the nearest object at hand — in this case, a table lamp with a frosted glass shade — and yanked it from its socket and threw it across the bar. It collided with the pinball machine and shattered to pieces.

For Touhey, that was the last straw. He grabbed Oi by the collar with his left hand, then, with his right, delivered two swift blows: with the first, I heard the appalling sound of Oi's nose splintering under the force of Touhey's fist; with the second, Oi's body went limp and fell backwards with a thud. He was out cold. Then Touhey grabbed Oi's feet, dragged his lifeless body out the door, and tossed it on the curb.

This altercation seemed to exhaust the last of Touhey's patience, because when he came back inside, he seemed just about ready to turn his anger on me.

"Unless you wanna end up like him," he said, casually wiping Oi's blood from his knuckles with a dirty bar towel, "I suggest you get a move on, too."

The Parade

AFTER GETTING KICKED out of the Tempus Fugit, I spent the next forty-five minutes searching for someone who could help Oi, or at least give him a ride to the hospital — but the only people out this late were not the helping kind, and every car I encountered sped up as soon as I tried to flag it down. Finally, I circled back to the bar, but when I got there, Oi was nowhere to be found.

At that point, I decided I might as well head over to The Bust's and try to get a couple hours' shut-eye. Unfortunately, by the time I made it to Patroon House, several official-looking types were running around making their final preparations for the parade. Without my knowledge, The Bust had appointed me to serve as his replacement. At least, I thought, he had been kind enough to lay out my costume before he left.

Almost delirious from exhaustion, I proceeded to dress myself in the itchy, brass-buttoned wool shirt and surprisingly narrow-waisted breeches, wondering how The Bust had ever expected to fit into an outfit that was uncomfortably tight even for me. Then, as if I didn't already look and feel ridiculous enough, I donned the white dickey, hobnail boots, and floppy fisherman's hat that completed the ensemble.

Returning downstairs, I discovered my old friend, the Rummy Mummy, back in his former position on the living room sofa, now dressed in a top hat, tails, and a bright purple sash that read, "Grand Marshal." Hoisting him back over my shoulder, I carried Jan outside and climbed up onto the horse-drawn carriage that was waiting out front. As you might imagine, we made for a pretty silly spectacle. But alas, the city had gone to great lengths to ensure a historic and momentous event, and nothing — not the loss of the *Good Woman*, not the sudden disappearance of The Bust, not my own sartorial scruples — was going to stand in the way of this parade.

Joining us was a motley assemblage of schoolchildren, church parishioners, civic club members, and other spirited Old Dutchers, split up into seven divisions, each representing a different era or aspect of the city's history. Setting out from Patroon House, our procession would ultimately bring us to a riverfront promenade, where a host of local luminaries would give speeches, offer toasts, and pose for photographs. Finally, when the sun began to set, fireworks would light up the sky.

As I waited to begin our march down Big Street, I felt as though I had never seen the city look so alive. If anything, the bounty of ornamentation already in place seemed to have increased overnight. Every building was now trimmed with bunting from top to bottom, and flags flew from every window. Looking toward the horizon, my vision was filled by an expanse of fluttering muslin, a vista in which all the colors of the rainbow intermingled freely. Though the total impression was somewhat garish, at least for once everything seemed to fit together. Even nature had decided to smile on us, providing clear skies and plenty of sunshine.

Before long, the citizens of Old Dutch began filling the sidewalk in droves. Always a rowdy and excitable bunch, today the locals were armed with confetti, noisemakers, and more than a few open containers of hooch. In trying to ban alcohol, The Bust seemed only to have strengthened his subjects' resolve to drink early and often.

I was wondering what he would have made of the crowd if he were here today, when who should suddenly come limping up to the carriage, leaning on a cane and dressed to the nines in period garb, but The Bust himself! He was wearing a sash across his chest that read, "Master of Ceremonies." Apparently, he hadn't had enough confidence in me to leave that particular bit of regalia behind.

"Good morning, Anselm," he said blasély.

"What are you doing here?" I asked, increasingly convinced that I was still asleep in my San Francisco apartment, and that this was all some deranged dream. "I thought you left town."

"Well, it's a funny story," he replied. "It wasn't until I got to the airport and started staring at the departures board that I realized I had absolutely no idea where I wanted to go. So I walked up to the ticket counter and asked when was the soonest flight I could buy tickets for. The lady told me that a plane for Atlanta would begin boarding in twenty minutes. Visions of the Braves, Ted Turner, Coca-Cola, and rap music danced through my head, and I thought, Atlanta! That's just the ticket! So I bought one, and the next thing I know I'm in Georgia.

"You can't really appreciate how hot it is in Atlanta until you've been there. And the humidity! As soon as I left the air conditioned comfort of the baggage claim and stepped outside, the sweat started rolling off me. Finally, after what felt like an eternity, I figured out where I could catch a cab and told the driver, 'Take me downtown!'

"Well, the driver just looked at me like I was nuts. I was thinking it would be like Old Dutch and you could just walk everywhere, but boy was I wrong! Everything was so spread out, so big, so new! I thought once we got to the city center, I'd just be able to pick a spot and ask the driver to let me out, but I couldn't make any sense of it. So finally I just chose some random street corner to get out and walk, but it was impossible to get my bearings.

"Soon I was so worn out by the heat and those long blocks that I decided to take a break and get something to eat. I stopped in at the first restaurant I found and tried ordering some Zippies or Riggies. But they had never heard of them! They had never even heard of Old Dutch City!

"I couldn't believe it. So I just started babbling on about my family, and Shytt Bergie and the Quadricentennial and even the Rummy Mummy, but the place was packed and the waiter only seemed interested in my order. Suddenly, I started to feel incredibly, overwhelmingly sad. Even my sandwich didn't seem as good as the ones we have here.

"At that point, all I wanted to do was get some sleep. So I got a room, switched on the TV, turned the AC on full blast, and promptly passed out. A few hours later, I was awakened by a throbbing headache and wave after wave of nausea. I realized that I was *literally* feeling homesick. It was then I knew that my place was here, at the parade. So now, here I am!"

"Welcome back," I replied. I didn't know what else to say. The Bust's ordeal in Atlanta strangely reminded me of my own experience upon returning to Old Dutch City. Suddenly, I realized that there was no longer any reason for me to be up on the carriage wearing this silly suit. "Want to switch places?" I asked hopefully.

"Fat chance!" The Bust answered. "Have fun, Anselm!" Then he limped back into the crowd, full of mirth and cheer.

Unfortunately, the Mummy and I weren't to be left alone for long. Soon, we were joined by a third, but I was still so baffled by The Bust's appearance that I didn't even notice her until she was sitting right next to me.

It was the girl from the Healing and Wellness Center! At first, this just confirmed my suspicion that I was dreaming the whole thing, until I realized that she, too, was wearing a sash. Only then did I finally realize where I had seen yesterday's guru before: she was none other than Miriam Van Eck, The Bust's little sister, the Pizza Princess herself!

"Mr. Kip," she said, smiling at me inscrutably. "What a pleasant surprise!"

It was certainly a surprise of some kind, I thought. I blushed and fidgeted in my seat, looking to the Mummy for support. I found none.

"What? Don't you recognize me, Anselm?" she asked.

"I do now," I said. "But I swear, when we...cured my halitosis yesterday, I had no idea that you were..."

"That I was what?" she replied, opening her eyes wide in an affected look of innocence.

"The Pizza Princess," I muttered.

It seemed I had struck a nerve, because as soon as I spoke those words Miriam grabbed me by the dickey, pulled me close, and whispered menacingly in my ear. "Never, ever, mention that again."

So that was how it was going to be. It occurred to me that my best bet was to change the subject, and fast. I started biting my fingernails nervously. "When does this thing get started?" I asked.

"Don't worry," she answered, "We're going last, so just sit back, smile, wave, and enjoy the show."

Finally, after what felt like the longest awkward silence of my life, a clamor of chimes and church bells, cries and car horns resounded across the city. The Quadricentennial was officially underway!

At the head of the parade was a brigade of street sweepers, comprised of old ladies wearing bonnets and peasant dresses. Wielding fat-bristled brooms and buckets of soapy suds, they fastidiously doused and scrubbed the grimy cobblestones. While the antics of these maids delighted the raving crowd, the slick cobblestones they left in their wake proved quite daunting to the *klompen* dancers who followed, dressed in clogs and aprons and kicking and stomping in unison: I saw one lady take a tumble, and another lose a clog. But both persevered and hobbled heroically on their way.

"Is this bringing back memories of how things used to be?" I asked the Mummy. He had no response.

Our boys in blue — thirty or so policemen marching admirably to fife and drum — comprised the second division. "Hey, it's my cousin Pete," I said, pointing to the most noticeably hungover of the officers.

"Of course you'd be related to Pete Kip," Miriam said. "That guy's a jerk."

I felt I ought to offer something in Pete's defense. "Well, I don't think so," I replied.

Old Dutch's modern police force was supplemented by a regiment of its representatives from days gone by, which included costumed constables, an ox-drawn cannon, and three mules with howitzers strapped to their backs. "I guess law enforcement tactics haven't changed much over the years," I joked.

"Please stop talking," answered Miriam, behind a forced smile.

Up next, on a convoy of flatbed trucks, was a series of *tableau vivants* depicting scenes of quotidian life in historical Old Dutch City. The first showed a cobbler mending loafers while a man reading a newspaper had his hair trimmed; the unevenness of the road had me worried that the scissors would slip and slice off one of the man's ears, but fortunately, the barber was a consummate professional.

Immediately following this scene came another, in which a man rolled off reams of leaflets with a hand-cranked printing press. As he passed our carriage, a few of his pages fluttered up to us, each bearing a different message:

Forever Float the Standard Sheet!
Use Self-Rising Flour — See the Results!
Coming Soon: Bread Pudding!

Son of a bitch! I turned back to give the printer a

closer look. That Van Dyke beard, that ruff collar, that sugar loaf hat — I could swear it was the same man who last night had claimed to be the Rummy Mummy! I turned to the real mummy sitting beside me. He seemed to be frowning.

On the next truck stood a red-shirted butcher plying his trade. While he hacked repeatedly into an indeterminate slab of meat, a fat hog and two cute piglets slumbered on the floor beside his counter, apparently undisturbed by the constant jolting over the pavement. The macabre nature of this scene proved too much for some, as it provoked uncontrollable crying from children all along the route.

Trailing the butcher was a commissariat wagon (where a dough-covered baker pulled loaves of bread from a wood-burning stove) hitched to a keg on wheels (where his assistant poured frothy pints for thirsty onlookers). Ignoring the constraints of my period garb, I jumped from the carriage, pushed my way through the swarming drunks, and grabbed a couple of beers for me and Miriam.

"Come on," I said, handing her a cup as I climbed back into the carriage. "It's a celebration!"

It didn't take much cajoling: she downed the entire thing in a single gulp.

Soon it would be our turn to join the parade, but first tribute had to be paid to Old Cock & Balls itself in the form of a giant float. Around flower sculptures of the corncob and the potato, arranged in the familiar fashion, a Dutchman bedecked in furs and a scantily-clad Indian brave posed, while a real live beaver scurried around the scene, obviously confused. It was definitely a sight to see! I was so taken with the inherent ribaldry of the tableau that I unconsciously started tickling Miriam's knee. Casually batting away my playful digits, she grabbed the reigns and gave them a couple of quick tugs. The carriage lurched onto Big Street and into the procession. We were on our way!

I took this as my cue to start smiling and waving like an idiot. I even lifted the Mummy's gnarly arm and made him wave, too. The crowd ate it up. As we approached a dais set up along the parade route, some guy with a microphone announced our approach.

"And last, but certainly not least," he cried, "we have our most honorable Grand Marshal, the one and only...Rummy Mummy!" At this, applause erupted such as I had never heard in my life. The way people were carrying on, I started worrying that they'd rush our carriage if we lingered too long. Finally I decided to present the Mummy to his adoring fans and hoisted his body into the air.

"Accompanying our illustrious Grand Marshal," the announcer continued, "is the lovely Miriam Van Eck. And seated beside here is...um...some guy!"

Hey! That's me, I thought. I'm some guy!

"Isn't that Anselm Kip?" I thought I heard someone say. Then, someone else seemed to add, "Way to go, Kip!"

And so our carriage inched its way down Big Street, greeted with every clop of its horses' hooves by a shower of whoops and cheers. Someone handed Miriam a bouquet of tulips, freshly ripped from the ground. The Rummy Mummy was doused in beer. Even I was given a few obligatory pats on the back, which I appreciated nonetheless. I almost wished it could go on forever, even as our terminus, the lavish grandstand where masters of oratory would consecrate this most glorious day, appeared in the distance.

The end, however, came sooner than expected, as a masked man riding a bicycle broke through a barricade, then came tearing up Big Street toward us, firing roman candles into the crowd. The bike weaved between the trucks and carriages, sparking a panic all along the route. The street sweepers scattered first, abandoning their brooms and crushing them under their stampeding feet, while the *klompen* dancers fled with the rest of the crowd, their retreat distinguished only by the continued stomping and kicking of their boots. Then, as their truck turned sharply to avoid hitting anyone, the barber tripped and inadvertently stabbed the cobbler, and the ensuing fracas awoke the butcher's pigs, causing them to leap to the street below and make a run for freedom. After that, the baker's oven exploded, shooting fiery loaves of bread flying through the air, and the only reason the conflagration wasn't worse was because the beer truck tipped over, too, spilling a flood of flat lager across the road that quelled the flames.

With police officers past and present hot on his heels, the rampaging cyclist finally pulled up beside our carriage, causing the horses to rear back in fright.

"Give me the Mummy, Kip!" he yelled. Though his face was hidden behind the traditional mask of the Lord of Misrule, I had no doubt it was Oi: he had the muted, nasally voice of a man with a broken nose.

"Never!" I shouted. It may seem a little melodramatic in retrospect, but at the time it seemed like an appropriate response.

Despite my opposition, Oi leaned into the carriage and grabbed hold of the Mummy's legs, while I kept my arms wrapped around his shoulders. Thus began an epic tug of war, in which I struggled to maintain my grip as Oi swerved back and forth on his bike and the horses bucked wildly, despite the best efforts of Miriam, who remained generally unperturbed, to calm them. Sadly, this battle was to have no winners: the Mummy's recent exposure to the elements had already weakened his leathery hide, and now, with all this jostling, his body had begun to split apart. All it took was one last determined tug from Oi, and the Mummy was ripped in two. Oi had managed to tear away the body's lower half, leaving me to cradle the Mummy's head and shoulders.

"Screw you, Kip!" cried Oi as he ran off into one of the abandoned buildings along the parade route. "I won't forget this!"

"Eww, gross," said Miriam, as she finally managed to bring the carriage to a halt. This was the first time she appeared at all interested in the battle that had been raging beside her. "Let me guess," she added. "Oisin Fitzpatrick."

I could only nod. Then, together, we turned to see where it was that Oi had escaped to.

It was Trencherman's.

O Oisin, Weep

As MIRIAM AND I stepped down from the carriage, the police struggled to establish a perimeter against stilted parade-goers who were hurling beer bottles and broomsticks at the abandoned restaurant. Miriam appeared delighted by the chaos.

"And people say Old Dutch City is boring," she said, smiling. "You sure you wanna leave?"

"The sooner, the better," I answered. Honestly, I didn't really care to find out what fate would befall Oisin. I just wanted to locate Pete, retrieve my suitcase, and get back home to my tiny, one-windowed apartment.

"So what are you going to do after all this?" I asked. "Are you going to try to salvage what's left of the Van Eck empire?"

She chuckled. "Doubtful. I think a change of scenery is in order. Perhaps I could go to San Francisco, help you with your plants."

"That would be nice," I admitted. "They could sure use it."

Suddenly, we realized that the mob was raging less violently than before and, looking up, saw that Oi had emerged from the same window where I had encountered him yesterday. Then I spotted Pete approaching the building holding a megaphone. "Oisin Fitzpatrick, we have you surrounded," he announced. "Come out with your hands up!"

Oi ignored the command. "Greetings, my subjects!" he declared, ducking an assault from a flying broomstick.

"Go to Hell!" cried more than one member of the crowd.

"The reign of the Van Ecks is over!" Oi proclaimed. "And I am your new King!"

"Suck my dick, Oisin!" yelled someone else.

"As your new King, my first act, is to reinstate the sale of alcohol, effective immediately. So stop whacking your willies and start tapping those kegs, because the time has come to toast this great city! Let's drink from sun down to sun up and to sun down again! Come all ye weirdos and rejoice!"

No one rejoiced.

"Cut the shit, Oisin!" Pete demanded. "Get down here now, or we're coming in after you."

"Wait, let me talk to him!" interjected The Bust, who had made his way to the front of the crowd. "Oisin, this is Anthony Van Eck speaking," he shouted.

"No one cares what you have to say, Bust," Oi replied.

"Listen, Oisin, I'm done fighting. Just come down here before you get hurt."

"Take a hike, fat ass."

At this, The Bust's tolerance for Oi's cartoonish vendetta reached its limit and he flew into a rage. Having failed with diplomacy, he now decided to give rocks a try. The Bust laid into his family's former restaurant with a vengeance, chucking whatever rubble was on hand with a force and velocity that he hadn't shown since his playing days. Soon, the entire crowd had joined in, and Miriam and I had to duck for cover to avoid falling debris as rocks ricocheted off of bricks, shattered windows, and cracked the building's molding.

"Go ahead, throw stones!" Oi screamed, as he tried (mostly unsuccessfully) to dodge the many projectiles hurled at him. "Tear down the city that I saved! While you let these buildings rot, I was the only one who heard them screaming: Remember me! Fill me! I'm empty inside, and no one cares!"

For these were ancient Oisin's fate
Loosed long ago from Heaven's gate,
For his last days to lie in wait.

The rocks continued to fly. Fixtures cracked and fell away. The facade of the building began to crumble.

O wandering Oisin,
The strength of the bell-branch is naught

"I've had enough," said Pete. "Get ready to move in." Members of the police force formed a tight line and began to march in lockstep toward the door. Even the costumed officers and the howitzer-wielding mules seemed eager to get in on the action.

For there moves alive in your fingers
The fluttering sadness of earth.

A low rumble began to emanate from the building.

"Hold your positions!" yelled Pete. "What the hell is that bastard up to now?"

Weep for your Niamh;
O Oisin, weep

The rumbling grew louder. Large chunks of plaster and brick fell to the pavement. Entire walls were giving way.

"Everyone get back!"

O Oisin, weep

And just like that, the building was gone.

THE END

About the Author

RYAN KITTLEMAN is an artist and writer living in San Francisco.

His paintings have been exhibited at the Crocker Art Museum, Morris Graves Museum of Art, and the Museum of Northern California Art, among others. Ryan's short film, *This Is How You Cry*, was screened in fourteen countries and won several awards, including at the L.A. Underground Film Forum, Cine Pobre Film Festival, and the Austin Arthouse Film Festival. In addition to *The High Cost of Macaroni*, Ryan has written one previous novel, *The Great Peace*, and a poetry collection called *The Honorable Mentions*.